"You've remembered something?" he asked

"But it's gone! It's gone!" There was an element of hysteria in Andrea's voice. She began to beat a small fist against his chest. "It was there, and it's gone!"

"Stop it now, little one. You can't tear yourself to pieces this way, Andrea." He shook her and her head lolled like a flower on a slender stalk. "Listen to me, Andrea, it will come back."

Her silence was a chilling, frightening thing. "You don't want me to remember, Steven. You told me."

"I've changed my mind," he said curtly. "I want you to remember Godden. You were his fiancée. You must have loved him."

"I didn't!" She hit him again in her agitation. "I don't know how I know, but I do. I didn't love him!"

MARGARET WAY
is also the author of these

Harlequin Presents

and these

Harlequin Romances

Many of these titles are available at your local bookseller.

For a free catalogue listing all available Harlequin Romances
and Harlequin Presents, send your name and address to:

HARLEQUIN READER SERVICE
1440 South Priest Drive, Tempe, AZ 85281
Canadian address: Stratford, Ontario N5A 6W2

MARGARET WAY

a man like daintree

Harlequin Books

TORONTO · LONDON · LOS ANGELES · AMSTERDAM
SYDNEY · HAMBURG · PARIS · STOCKHOLM · ATHENS · TOKYO

Harlequin Presents edition published January 1975
ISBN 0-373-15040-7

Second printing October 1977
Third printing March 1979
Fourth printing April 1982

Original hardcover edition published in 1972
by Mills & Boon Limited

CHAPTER I

SHE was alone. All alone in a . . . *rain jungle*, yet its beauty
seemed to compensate for all else. Forest giants ringed her
round, hurtling straight up towards the cobalt chinks of
light in a fierce competitive battle for sun and supremacy,
wreathed in parasitic vines, the strangling rope-like lianas
that twisted and intertwined and made bridgeways for a
teeming nocturnal population.

She was lying on her back in the centre of a small clearing of luxuriant ferns and orchid-like growths of a peculiar
fantasy and beauty; creamy and yellow-gold perfection
speckled with bronze and cerise and brown velvet. It was
deathly still, so still she could scarcely breathe. Not a
breeze pierced the thick canopy of trees, burdened with
nesting birds, gorgeous with fleeting glimpses of colour.

She swallowed weakly and gagged a little, reassured by
that densely blue patch of sky framed by the leaves. A
strange, iridescent insect with huge gauzy wings flitted
along her arm. She tried to brush it away but couldn't.
Something was wrong with her arm, but she was in no
pain, anaesthetized by shock. Her mind was completely
placid, not a ripple to corrugate its unquestioning sur-
face. She tried to turn her head, suffering an unexpected
dizzying sense of vertigo, seeking to pierce the high forest galleries its shadowy depths, but it all seemed to close
in on her in a swirling, tangled mass of virulent green.

Red lights danced in front of her eyes and a film of
sweat broke out on her face. Something warm trickled
down her temple to slide sickly along her cheek. Her eyes
fastened, without horror, on a snake. It *was* a snake, or

perhaps even a python, enormously long, beautifully marked, gleaming, gliding in a sinuous trail along the interlacing lianas, festooned with red blossom. She had no fear, nothing rendered incapable of even a quiver of revulsion. The snake continued on its deadly business lost in a dazzle of moving greenery.

The next time she came around it was to fear and pain; a panic that grew in intensity until her mind reeled, disorientated, terror-stricken. Where was she? What was happening? Was she dead or alive or in the middle of some loathsome nightmare? Her mind juggled frantically, out of control. The whole inky black night was going round in a spin, alive with rustlings and queer noises that made her hair stand on end. Shadows came up to her to vanish again. A night bird gave a hoarse, melancholy call and she plunged up convulsively, to sink back in a stupor of pain, fighting to retain consciousness. A ceaseless hum dinned into her eardrums – mosquitoes. Millions of them, bombarding her tender skin with ravenous appetite. She was a flaming mass of pain, red-hot needles jabbing into the satiny exposed flesh.

"God! God!"

The tempo of pain increased in her hand, exploding in a dull red roar. She turned her head frantically, uncontrollably, aggravating her wound, losing consciousness until relapse drew her terror to a close.

This time she roused to a dream world. Great billowy clouds sailed above the tree-tops, changing from rose to gleaming gold. Shafts of early morning sunlight streamed down the narrow walls of the jungle, colouring her world greeny-golden. Continuous bird calls carolled from tree-top to tree-top, ringing the forest round, alive with the darting flashes of brilliant plumage; the flame of crimson and scarlet, deepest, unbelievable blue, bright yellow, and purple. The banks of orchid-like growths had a heavy, exotic perfume, almost soporific. She felt better, or she imagined she felt better, but inexpressibly weak.

She lay on her back for perhaps an hour or so with the seeming indolence of physical malaise, watching the dappled dazzle pattern of sun and shade through the lustrous greenery. Suddenly a big bird, a blue crane, flashed into sight, winging low over the tangled shrubbery, leaving the echo of its strange, metallic call. Her white forehead pleated, losing something of its pathetic inertia. A slow excitement seemed to burn along her veins. A blue crane — a brolga! Somewhere there must be water. Hope surged through her numbed body, a return of the priceless, enduring spirit, the will to live. Some dreadful catastrophe had brought her to this place. She had no recollection of what, no insidious questions clamoured in her brain. That way lay insanity. It would all come back, in time. She could die a hundred deaths, yet live to die again in this beautiful, terrifying place. Fate might have been less cruel.

A curly frond reached out to caress her face, creeping fingers that touched her arm and shoulders. She looked down along the length of her body — a slender, finely boned body. She was wearing a sand-coloured shirt and cotton slacks, or they might once have been sand-coloured. The right sleeve of her shirt had been torn out, a great rent at the knee of her slacks. She tried to raise her right arm, wincing with pain. It was very swollen a few inches above the wrist, but the arm itself was not out of shape. She was certain there were bones broken.

In the next half hour she made numerous attempts to get up and finally stood swaying like a leaf in a storm. Incredible that it should be so, but her strength had been taken from her. Struggling to keep her feet, she clutched out at a palm frond, only to have cut a ribbon of blood along her palm. Pain sobered her, collecting her swimming senses. With a little courage she could defy the jungle labyrinths, cheat them of one more death. Somewhere there was water. She must find it. The brolga had shown her the way. Water was life – in the desert, in the jungle. Along the waterways there was hope, perhaps human habitation. The conviction grew in her that she would be saved, without logic or reason, an intuitive thing. She was drained of all emotion. There was no power in her to feel anything – sorrow, fear, only a stoic indifference, even to pain. A stray beam of sunlight caught the coppery sheen of a little gold medallion she wore round her neck. *St. Christopher*, she interpreted it, but not for many long weeks afterwards could she remember who had given it to her.

CHAPTER II

WHAT drove him on? He didn't know. It was four days now since the light aircraft had been reported missing, three since the scattered wreck had been sighted. Two days since the charred remains of the young man had been brought in for burial. The girl was still missing and this was wild bush, true rain jungle. She hadn't a hope in hell, even if she was alive. Yet something kept at him; a subdued kind of glow almost like a candle of hope. Maybe the girl held it. He shrugged his powerful shoulders, more cynical than compassionate, a big man, hard, self-reliant, skin tanned to teak from a tropical sun, his jet black head uncovered.

If the girl was alive he would find her. He hadn't much time for women beyond their obvious accomplishments, but this was suffering humanity. Besides, he knew the jungle if anyone did. He had some grasp of its enormous complexities. He'd been born on its fringe; explored it during a boyhood spent in the Never-Never with his father, *Byamee*, as the myalls called him, *one plenty white fella* – Garth Daintree, one of the Gulf Country's real identities; a beef cattle pioneer. Now he, Steven Daintree, ran his own herds on the neighbouring tablelands, adding to his father's great selection with one of his own – Mokhana, a cattle station of the future.

His palms were badly calloused and blistered from work with the machete. It was hard going even for him. He wiped the sweat from his head and made a vow to himself; if he didn't find her by nightfall he would have to give up. There were others in the field with fewer res-

9

ponsibilities. God alone knew if he was on the right track, but it was more than a calculated hunch. If the girl had any bush sense at all she would head for a stream. *He* knew them all. His dark face hardened. But what if she had no sense at all? Injured, very probably, and terrorised by the jungle. What was her name? Andrea, that was it. A silly, silky soft, feminine sort of name. One he'd expect. Just another pretty face hiding a yawning vacuity.

Andrea Swanson, aged twenty-two, on route from Brisbane to Cairns, thirteen hundred miles away, with her fiancé, Carl Godden, one of the *sugar* Goddens, with the wealth of a half a dozen plantations behind them. Twenty-two! Not much more than a kid. His chiselled mouth softened barely perceptibly. Twenty-two to his thirty-six. If she was alive she'd have some grief-stricken months ahead of her. Like the boy's family. Irina Godden, the mother, had collapsed when the news had been broken to her and was still under sedation. Nick Godden, the shrewd and hard-headed business man, had broken down at an interview he himself had called. He had other sons, yes, but this was his youngest. There was no need now to remember the endless arguments with Irina, his wife, who had pampered and indulged and was so foolishly proud of their playboy son. The boy was dead, eighteen months older than the girl they had never met.

Daintree released his blade and slashed at a lawyer vine, slicing it downwards in one savage chop. He'd heard plenty of stories about young Godden. None of them mattered now except that if the girl ran true to type she wouldn't be able to fend for herself outside of the charmed circle of luxury and being waited on hand and foot. The heavy shrub closed in on him and he manoeuvred sideways, avoiding a snake that slithered apprehensively away from his sword arm.

The jungle was a frightening place and she had spent three nights in it. *If* she was alive. He gave himself a few moments' respite, then hacked on with what might have seemed in another man a kind of desperation. He was covered in sweat, his arms specked with blood from jagged leaf cuts and thorn stabs but standing squarely on his feet with forty-eight sleeplesss hours behind him.

In another hour he came down on the creek his father had once called Camp One. A gigantic eagle was soaring above it, screeching in baffled rage. The hairs on the back of his neck prickled and stood up. Something whispered to him fiercely: *This is it! This is it!* The critical moment had come. He was poised almost rigid, wiping the sweat from his brow with the back of his hand, letting his eyes roam over the musky, dank glade. His pent-up breath was expelled on a harsh, whistling sigh.

She was lying outstretched against a flat boulder, her arms gently floated open, one hand clutching a clump of white lilies, her long silvery fair hair trailing like sea silk in the stream. A ghostly light enshrouded her, a kind of deathly trance. Her beauty was eerie, heartbreaking. She looked like a beaten child, bleeding hands and feet, lacerated by the tearing thorns and clinging vines that had put him through a living hell, and him with a machete! Her face was miraculously untouched, a gleaming alabaster, like the lilies that grew in profusion along the reed flats.

He felt a knife-thrust of bitterest defeat. Nausea moved in him and into his mouth came an acrid taste. This was a dead girl. She was not alive at all, only a shell, a beautiful shell that had only briefly glimpsed life. The horror and the pity of it! He could have taken it better had she been a man. Instinct alone guided his body in its swift, impeccable descent. He felt no weight, no gravitation, branches whipping about his waist, flailing him, but he never felt it.

He jerked to a halt under the weirdest illusion that one of her hands seemed to clench and slowly unclench. He could see now the wound high up on her temple. Blood that had once oozed from it had long since matted to her pale hair. He moved towards her with a dreadful sureness, a deliberation of purpose that was unmistakable. Mind, the prime master, had taken over from his physical reaction to the shock of discovery. The body would have to be taken back. She was dead. Young, beautiful. She had courage and had proved it, but now she was dead.

He bent over her. There was a lambent quality to the satiny skin, a queerly greenish tinge. He wanted to leave her at peace with her lilies. She looked barely more than a child with her white innocent brow. He slipped a hand inside her shirt, feeling her slight breast with an icy chill off the skin. His hand lay over her heart and a flash of triumph turned his eyes glittery. The high badge of courage was often rewarded. The heartbeat was weak, but it was there, softly thudding, the all-vital life force. He ran his badly blistered hands with exquisite gentleness over her long, youthful limbs. One arm was certainly broken. There were multiple minor injuries, savage mosquito bites, some on her legs already infected. The wound on her head could be bad. There was a tiny trickle of blood near her mouth that had him worried because he didn't know for sure where it came from. If it was from her mouth it spoke of internal injury. He touched his fingers to both sides of her soft mouth. No sign of blood there, but she had to be treated at once.

He moved to the centre of the clearing and removed his revolver from its shoulder holster, sending a volley of shots into the air – three for dead, four for alive. The forest echoed and re-echoed, reverberating for miles around, swirling the birds in frenzied, jewel-coloured masses, screeching their protests to the high heavens, scattering a myriad spent blossoms like tongues of flame. If he went back the way he had come he would reach the rescue party in the near vicinity before they could get to him. *If* they could even find the trail. He didn't want to shift her, but he had to risk it. There was no place at all for a chopper to set down.

He sheathed his revolver and turned back to the girl. Incredibly her eyes were open, the soft translucent grey of a dawn sky. The quality of their expression caught at some vulnerable spot in him, one he never knew he still had.

"Hello!" she said in a phantom voice that might vanish at a breath, leaving its tremulous echo floating on the air. He bent towards her without speaking, his brooding gaze swept over her ivory face. "Don't leave me," she whispered. "I've been . . . so *alone!*" Her tongue touched her parched mouth.

He turned away to drench a handkerchief at the stream, beading her face and mouth with moisture. His voice was a dark undertone, low-keyed, almost emotionless:

"You're safe, quite safe. I have you now."

She stared up at the hard planes of his face, enchained by a will-power far superior to her own. It was the face of a statue, carved in bronze, a sombre, arrogant face, the cut of the nostrils, the curve of the handsome mouth, hard and imperious. The eyes were a shock, the only moving thing in that dark, carved stillness; a brilliant ever-changing blue-green.

"Promise me nothing will go wrong. Not now!" She fought her way out of the mist that was growing in front of her eyes, directly holding his jewelled glance. "*Can* one

13

exact promises from a statue?"

He had to bend his dark head to catch that strange little phrase frightened by the extreme pallor of her face. She might think him a statue, but he had saved her life. Some time she would have to remember it even if he wanted no thanks. A little warmth seemed to have seeped into her slight body. He cradled her in his arms easily, taking her weight, scrupulously avoiding hurting her swollen arm, and thanked the gods the return route had been robbed of so many of its tortures. This child had had enough. Her heavy lashes lay still on her cheeks. He bent his dark head over her face to protect her white skin from the sun and the heat, the inevitable whiplash some branch would bring, the spray of leaves and twigs that leapt in the air. With any luck she should live – live to make a fool and a slave of some weak-willed man. A woman's beauty, in its way, was an invincible weapon.

In complete silence, intensely preoccupied, he made his way back through the jungle, bearing his burden, to emerge from the trees and into the open savannah. Force Two of the rescue squad greeted him with waves and shouts, a uniform eagerness that shone as relief on their tired, dark-stubbled faces. A light aircraft circled their heads preparatory to land. He scarcely seemed aware of their combined clamour of congratulations for a superb physical feat, standing guard over the girl until the Flying Doctor Service put down.

It took young Doctor Freedman from Tempe Downs Base Hospital to sum it up neatly with a certain wry grin:

"I guess a man like Daintree could do anything. At any rate he reached her in time. She'll live!"

With her eyes tightly shut she could visualise a face, a remote, darkly sculptured face, with a kind of hard perfection on it, like a statue. Only the eyes were open, not shut. Not black as one might have expected, but a coldly brilliant, blue-green, almost aquamarine. It was a familiar yet utterly unfamiliar face. For the life of her she couldn't place it. An increasing panic grew in her and she flung out her hand.

A firm cool hand clamped around her wrist. She gave a shuddering start and opened her eyes. She was in a high, narrow bed in a strange room. It was light, airy, with sunlight streaming through open windows, the sun-wind fluttering the curtains, yet it was filled with the unmistakable clinical odour of a hospital. A stocky, pleasant-faced young woman dressed in a nurse's uniform with a white cap firmly anchored to her curls stood beside the bed. She was holding her wrist to check the pulse rate. A smile came into her warm, brown eyes.

"Awake, are you? How do you feel?"

"Wonderful!" The large grey eyes, faintly tilted at the corners, roamed around the room with a look of mild interest.

The older girl smiled. "Well, that's the sort of answer one might expect from a heroine. *Wonderful!* Imagine!" She sounded as if she was storing the word up for later retelling.

"A heroine? Not me," the girl said gravely. She took a deep, slow breath as if to clear her head of all its butterfly thoughts.

"Well, *I* think so!" the little nurse protested. "And plenty of other people tend to think the same way. Of course, Mr. Daintree brought you in."

"Daintree?" The girl looked up at her with wide, curiously smouldering eyes.

"Yes, Steven Daintree. He owns Mokhana, you know. He's a big man in our part of the world, as I expect you know. Now lie back, dear, and I'll check the dressing on

15

your head. That was a nasty blow. I'll try not to hurt you."

"Don't worry!" A small smile glided across the girl's mouth at some private thought.

The nurse looked down at those, clean, finely boned features, wishing not for the first time that she was a cool blonde. Everything seemed to happen to them. Not only the good things, of course. She grew vaguely ashamed of her thoughts and smiled.

"Doctor Freedman will be looking in presently. He's quite pleased with your progress. I imagine he'll be wanting to have a little chat with you. You've been out most of the time."

"A little chat? About what?"

"Oh, this and that," the nurse replied, purposely off-hand. She stared down at the girl with eyes that were anything but off-hand, then changed the subject to say brightly:

"What beautiful hair you've got! A true silver-gilt. I have a little niece with hair like this, but I didn't think it survived childhood. The funny part is, her mother – my sister, you know – wanted to call her Andrea. But Bob, the father, that is, insisted on calling the poor little mite Hilary, after his mother. Nance named the other four. Imagine burdening a kid with a name like Hilary!" The grimace sounded in her laughing voice.

The girl in the bed looked up at her apprehensively almost. "I rather like it. Is *that* my name . . . Andrea?"

The little nurse blinked. "Of course, dear. What else? Andrea Swanson. Don't tell me you can't remember?"

"No, I can't!" The soft, musical voice fell almost flat.

"Well, never mind!" the nurse said bracingly. "You've had a bad time of it, goodness knows. I expect it will all come back in a day or two." A frown was gathering be-

16

tween her dark brows.

"I hope so!" the girl agreed quietly.

"Can you remember anything else?" the nurse asked after a moment of consideration.

"I remember the man who found me!"

"Who wouldn't?" The gentle ministering hands were almost through. Her deft, capable hands were behind her patient, lifting her, straightening her pillows.

"You know Mr. Daintree?" The blonde girl turned her head catching the other's deprecating grin.

"No, worse luck! I've seen him plenty of times, but I can't actually say I've met him. Steven Daintree moves in different circles, I can tell you. He's kind of inaccessible, to us mere mortals, but terribly good-looking, if you like that kind of thing. Dark and forbidding, and those eyes! – the glitter of them is enough to give you the shivers!" She broke off, blushing a little, obviously regretting her outburst. The girl seemed scarcely to have heard her tracing long pale fingers over the cast on her arm.

"Has he been to the hospital?"

"No, dear. He's gone back to Mokhana. That's his cattle station. One of the best in the State," she said proudly, getting a vicarious kick out of it. "Dr. Freedman reports on your progress, though, I understand."

"Oh!" The girl's voice was suddenly faint and far-off, completely uninterested.

"And now you're drowsy," the nurse said sympathetically. "I'll leave you in peace. My name's Susan Harris. I expect you'll be seeing a good bit of me. Now have a little nap. Doctor Freedman is still doing his rounds. Just lie back and relax."

She gave a cheerful, professional little nod of her head and went out of the room briskly, shutting the door.

Lie back and relax! She repeated the words soundlessly

17

over and over. They didn't seem to make much sense, not for a girl whose recollection of her life was an unsolved mystery. She turned her head into the pillow. It would be futile to lash out at fate. She breathed deeply, long, slow breaths, until the sick, lost sensation passed. She had come through all right. She had so much to be thankful for. Everything would come right, she repeated to herself jaggedly. Daintree would tell her what she must do, as calmly dispassionate as a judge. He would tell her what she needed to know. She was sure of it without knowing why. She was too tired to reason these things out. For the first time a quiver of emotion touched her soft, sensuous mouth. She sighed deeply, pressed back into the cool mound of pillows and closed her eyes.

A shadow fell across the bed. She opened her eyes empty of all but drowsy curiosity, a spasm of pain, seeing him at first in profile: a young man in a white coat studying a chart. He had a thick rather unruly thatch of toffee-coloured hair, a nose that had certainly been broken, an incisive mouth and a no-nonsense chin. He turned and smiled, and when the smile came full on he was an attractive man with light blue eyes sparkling, his manner easy and unruffled.

"How goes it, Miss Swanson?" He didn't wait for her answer but bent over her, pressing down the skin under her eyes and staring into her pupils. "Any headache?"

"Yes, rather a bad one."

He flicked his cuff back over his wrist watch and took her pulse. It was slow but not dangerously so. In his experience, her behaviour since she had been admitted had been abnormally quiet. Victims of a deep concussion were usually uninhibited, sometimes embarrassingly so, yet all this girl's recorded ramblings centred around her experience in the jungle and her recollections of Steven Dain-

18

tree. She was far too restrained and he could only guess at her normal temperamental pattern. He looked directly at her and she was obliged to return his gaze.

"Nurse tells me you have a small problem?"

"I can't remember my name." She was surveying him with great gravity out of her large grey eyes. Her intentness and complete unconsciousness of herself underlined her beauty and for a moment his normal processes of professional routine were wholly arrested. His reaction was purely masculine and aesthetic. She was, he concluded, in a blonde, remote way, the most beautiful human creature he had ever laid eyes on, the body as cleanly cut and faultless as the face. Her grave eyes disturbed him and made him speak more briskly than he intended.

"Do you *want* to remember it?"

"Of course!"

"Then you will. Do you realise you were involved in a plane crash? Light aircraft." He pulled up a chair and sat down beside the bed, waiting for her answer.

She looked back at him with a semblance of shocked surprise and winced a little. "It may seem odd, but I haven't been curious . . . of *anything*!"

His eyes sharpened. "You have no recollection of it?"

"None at all. It's as if my life began in the rain forest, the trees and the birds and the banks of orchids."

He had read a lot of this on her case sheet. He drew his brows together. "It's temporary amnesia, of course," he said quietly, "but I don't want you to be frightened by a name. It's nothing, I promise, to worry you. You just have to give yourself a little time."

"*How* long?" she asked in a faintly weary abstracted tone.

"I can't say. I didn't consider this new development. Now I must. You've been through a bad time. We must

19

be patient. The extent of the concussion was rather bad but the blow itself not all that serious – no fractures, no sign of real damage, no deeper injury below. You have a broken arm which should soon mend with your nice clean bones. You're still in a state of shock to a certain extent. Sometimes the mind seeks a refuge just as the body does."

Her eyes were uncanny, great shadowed pools of light. "What happened to the others? The pilot, the passengers?"

"There were no other passengers," he said soberly. "Only yourself. The pilot was killed."

"Oh, I'm so very sorry!" Her reaction was no more than a quick instinctive compassion and regret. Her eyes were widely fixed on his face. "I suppose I'm lucky to be alive!"

"Very lucky!" he agreed with studied calm. "But for Daintree we'd all but given up hope. You were a long way from the wreckage."

She flinched and his voice trailed away. He waited a little for some indications of disturbance, but none came. She was a snow princess locked away in her ivory tower, with her still, pale face and silvery hair.

"Do you want to hear a little about yourself, Andrea?" he asked gently.

"I suppose so!" A faint quiver of humour touched her mouth. A heartening sign. "My name is Andrea Swanson . . ."

". . . aged twenty-two," he took up. "You came out from England with your parents when you were four years old and settled in Melbourne. Your mother died ten years later, then you and your father came up to Queensland to a warmer climate. I understand your father wasn't a well man. He died less than six months ago. He saw to it that you had a good education. You teach English litera-

20

ture and history at a well-known girls' school." He looked down at her and his serious expression relaxed. He gave an encouraging smile. "Any of this mean anything to you?"

She plucked at the top sheet rather distractedly. "I'm sorry, but no." She hesitated for a moment, then looked up at him. "Could I see myself? I don't even know what I look like!"

He was shocked by the stark fear in her eyes, her first real show of emotion. He answered swiftly, warmly:

"Your face is unmarked. You're a beautiful girl, Andrea, and you've still got your English complexion. I'll get Nurse Harris to bring you a mirror. She can get you some cosmetics, whatever you like. Just tell her."

She bowed her head. The sight of her own face might jolt her memory, surely?

"I have no money, have I?" she asked rather helplessly.

He drew a deep breath almost of reprieve. "That's all been taken care of. We've had plenty of offers to look after you, as a matter of fact, but we decided to accept the first."

"Mr. Daintree?" she asked, her voice a silvery thread hanging in the warm air.

"Right in one!" he answered laconically, but for the life of him he couldn't manage a brighter tone. His mouth softened at the expression in her eyes. "I wouldn't worry about it, Andrea. Steven Daintree has more of this world's possessions than he'll ever need."

"It's kind of him, all the same," she insisted.

"Kind?" He seemed to savour the word and find it inadequate. He forced a smile. "It's certainly typical. A man like Daintree doesn't leave strings untied. He found you, he'll see you on your feet." His keen eyes did not

21

miss her slight agitation. That couldn't be allowed. "Now I'm going to give you something to make you sleep. Complete rest is what you need. Your brain is functioning quite normally except for this defensive block it seems to have put up. I'll put it this way – you've survived an ordeal; now with adequate rest, good food and attention everything else should click into place."

Her mouth quivered, then was still. "I'll have to take your word for it. Are you sure I don't need a psychiatrist instead of a doctor?"

He shook his head in sharp contradiction, sending a quick probing look into her lake-coloured eyes. "Quite sure. You've been badly concussed and shocked, so something of this nature is not altogether unusual. Perhaps you'll wake up to find you've remembered everything." He turned away for a moment, not wanting to meet her eyes, test her powers of belief. He came back to her and swabbed her arm. "Now this is only a pinprick. Close your eyes and remember you're safe and among friends."

She turned her head away from the needle, her eyelids fluttering obediently as if she were already on the borderline of sleep. "That's what *he* said," she murmured faintly. "You're safe. Quite safe . . ."

He stared down at the pure oval of her face, feeling not compassion but conflicting sensations that filled him with a general sense of guilt and irritation. He had some deep-seated concern for this girl, some niggling worry that he couldn't put a finger to. Strange, but she was fast developing a psychological dependence on Daintree, the harmful delusion that he was some kind of saviour. Somehow in her pitiful need for reassurance he stood as a link between her past and her future. Whatever happened to her now was partly – no, essentially – what Daintree would dictate.

He had a sharp mental picture of the man. Proud as Lucifer. Powerful, ambitious, completely self-orientated. Certain men, he was forced to concede, had the power to take hold of the mind, the imagination. Some link had been forged between Daintree and the girl by some strange circumstance of fate. Even Daintree when he brought her in appeared to have been shaken out of his monumental calm and indifference, though it was now firmly back in place. The doctor passed a hand over his face almost wearily. It was impossible to assess the result of this chance encounter. Around Daintree hung the aura of dynamism, wordly success. He didn't like the man, he was too impersonal, but he had to admire his wholly adult, driving brain. *And* he was anything but tight-fisted with his "loose change", as any legitimate charity would have to acclaim. What *was* it that bothered him? From all accounts, Daintree was no woman-hater, but he was said to regard them no higher than passing distractions. Doctor Freedman turned sharply towards the bed. This child with her sensitive face and long delicate bones stood to be hurt – badly. Daintree was that kind of man. Any woman save one of his own kind would do well to avoid him.

All at once tiredness attacked him, an odd sense of flatness. For a moment he considered withholding this new development from the man, then decided against it. It would be unwise, to say the least, at a time when plans for a new wing were in the offing. In any event he wouldn't be able to hold the Goddens off for more than a few days, and by that time she might remember their son. He gave a funny deep sigh of exasperation. Irina Godden would be a problem. He was not at all sure this child could withstand the battering rams of grief and hysteria that Irina Godden might subject her to. The tangled

23

web of fate! A fate that had deprived a spoilt, over-indulged woman of her beloved son, leaving her clinging to those last moments that could only be supplied by a stranger, a young woman, whom her son had loved and wanted to bring home. Lord knows it was difficult enough to remain completely emotionally detached from the girl himself.

He looked down at her face. It seemed cruel to awaken her, but she would have to be watched carefully from now on for any further sign of mental impairment. These head injuries were the devil, even when they appeared to be superficially imposed. She looked neat and clean and very young in her dreamless calm, her brows and lashes darkly emphatic against her white skin. She didn't look at all the type he imagined young Godden would have been interested in, but then again, one could never tell about these things. She was beautiful enough to ensnare any man.

A tap on the door broke into his speculations. He turned with feigned geniality to see Nurse Harris standing in the doorway with conscious professional poise.

"Mr. Daintree on the line, sir!"

His eyes seemed to look through and beyond her as if something had conquered all his attentions. Just as he thought he might relay a message to Daintree here was the man himself. Ah well, there was nothing else for it; a situation must not be allowed to develop. Within seconds he was his usual cool, unruffled self, giving Nurse Harris some brief, concise instructions, walking along the polished wood corridor to his office at the end of the wing.

The voice on the telephone matched the man; dark-timbred, direct, diabolically self-assured.

"Daintree here!" It came over very crisp and distinct. Then it was his turn, the faintest patch of colour staining his cheekbones, put there by the humiliating but probably erroneous impression that Steven Daintree had judged him and found him wanting as a man ... as a medic. He fought his own mingled resentments and embarked on a professional routine, giving the facts and the risks, over-explaining, if anything, but then that was the damnable effect Daintree had on him – almost, he thought, with a rush of self-disgust, like the nervous volubility of an inferiority complex.

Daintree cut through his wordy exposition.

"I'd like to see her!"

The doctor hesitated for a fraction of a second, trying to determine whether there was a faintly hostile element in the question. "Today?"

"Of course today!" The distinctive voice became, if anything, even more distinct. "I've flown in especially for that purpose."

Damn the man! Freedman thought irritably. He seemed to possess a prestige and authority that was entirely natural and unmistakable. Reacting perversely, he decided to argue the point over. "I don't think that would be wise. Tomorrow, the day after, perhaps!" He sounded vaguely pontifical even to his own ears, almost helpless to change anything.

The line fairly crackled, electric with unconcealed impatience.

"Damn it all, Freedman, I'm not a relative! I'm not going to excite or upset the girl. In the normal course of events, I'd be prepared to defer your judgement, but this case is different, especially in view of this new development. It has to be today. I'm sure you understand!" The cool urbanity was back in the voice again, inflexible as honed steel. Steven Daintree would be a hard man to toss under any circumstances. There was a cold, rigid pause and Freedman was forced into breaking it, feeling a certain dismayed contempt for his own sensations, based as they were on emotions, not logic. In all fairness to the man, Daintree could be depended upon to know how to act in a sickroom. He became equally courteous.

"Very well then, as you wish, Mr. Daintree. We'll expect you this afternoon."

"Thank you, Doctor." Steven Daintree hung up suavely on the last word, leaving Freedman to yet another small crisis in this day-to-day life. As usual he resolved it with a cigarette, smiling wryly at thoughts of possible lung damage but clinging to his self-delusions. He had no other vices he would admit to. After a few moments of thought-crowded contemplation he turned away to the steel cabinet that held the recent X-ray photographs. He riffled through them to the letter S, then took out the girl's and held them up to the light. Now that he looked again there was a faint something which could be a very fine frontal crack. Equally well it might not. Any rate, it wasn't anything dangerous. The girl was maintaining her condition – no, improving it. She was quite rational. The temporary amnesia was not entirely unexpected. He would look in again on her before Daintree arrived.

As it happened he was tied up with a veritable epidemic of casualties for the rest of the day, anything from snakebite to badly jaundiced babies. Nurse Harris found herself with the privilege of escorting *the* Steven Daintree along to the east wing and the private rooms that opened off the polished wood corridor. Daintree was conscious of the little darting feminine glances that came his way only to withdraw every time he turned his head, but otherwise her manner was as sweetly professional as a nurse in a T.V. series, he observed with a certain tolerant contempt.

He had no time for the coy female manoeuvres. Something about the whole Swanson business was gnawing at him like an aching joint. Irina Godden had already contacted him twice to thank him for the part he had played in the girl's rescue, taking a strangely proprietorial line more fitting to a close relative than a virtual stranger. She seemed all set to transfer a crushing mother love. Ah well, it was none of his business. The sooner the girl was on her feet and able to look after herself the better. Perhaps she'd be glad of a free meal ticket with the Goddens since she had no money herself, no family now since her father died. He shrugged his powerful shoulders almost in rejection. He was far too busy for this kind of thing. As he had explained to Freedman, he wasn't a relative. The girl had no claim on him even if he had saved her life.

Inside Room 8B the patient was sleeping, her face turned into the pillows. Those fine bones he remembered had a look of chiselled impersonality. It wasn't a face at all but a vacant mask of beauty, empty and forlorn. Something stirred in him, making him turn on the little nurse. He looked a very, very formidable man.

"You might tell Dr. Freedman I'm here!"

She stared up at him, startled by his arrested movement, and flushed at his tone, thoroughly disconcerted.

"Why, certainly, Mr. Daintree!"

Slavery is abolished, Steven Daintree, she thought, inwardly ruffled by the glitter off those uncanny eyes. This was a complete reversal of their positions. *She* was the one connected with the hospital, even if he had endowed a ward that was named after his father.

He read her thoughts easily. "It's quite all right, Nurse," he said smoothly, and she flushed anew at his

27

sudden transforming white smile. He moved to the door with her with lithe grace. "No fuss, no bother. Just run along and report."

"Certainly, Mr. Daintree," she repeated rather breathlessly, wondering if everyone he came in contact with toed the line. She was flushed to the point of her starched white collar. These men they thought they could use their strength and personality to bend you to anything! She shuddered a little. Steven Daintree might be a strikingly handsome man, but he would give a woman *hell*! One didn't need to be an expert to see that. Inwardly flustered, outwardly serious, she made her way back along the corridor, recollecting she should have remained with her patient, but Dr. Freedman *did* say he wanted to be informed of the great man's arrival.

Inside Room 8 Daintree looked down at the sleeping girl. His eyes were searching, not liking what he saw, although with nothing concrete to go on but a feeling. He narrowed his eyes against the reflected glare of the sun that turned her ash-gold hair to a living shield. He turned away to adjust the blinds, then moved back and sat down on the white wooden chair, moving it nearer the bed.

A spasm of pain seemed to move across those still features. She reached up a fumbling hand to the dressing on her head. He caught it and put it firmly aside.

"Don't *do* that!" she said with painful emphasis.

Her eyes were firmly closed, the lashes densely bunched. He tried to withdraw his hand, but her fingers were locked on his own, with surprising strength. He looked down at that palely clenched hand with its long tapering fingers and fine, oval-shaped nails and his thoughts were disrupted by an increasing aura of uneasiness, the faint prickles of awareness akin to those moments of danger when he was out game hunting on the tidal estuaries. There was something wrong here, a warning antenna. Yet why should he think it? Freedman's report was reassuring enough, discounting the amnesia bit. It wasn't the first time he had heard of a temporary memory block. He exerted the faintest pressure of his own and the girl relaxed her frantic grip. Her lips parted and her eyes flew open.

"Oh, it's you!" she said with difficulty, touching the tip of her tongue to her mouth. Her eyes were enormous, shimmering lakes of pain and tension, silvery grey. The fixed stare left them as she slowly refocused.

"How are you?" he asked quietly.

Her eyes seemed drawn to him fascinated, staring at him as though there was a special rhythm, a meaning to his features. "I feel dreadful. My head aches!"

"I know."

She was as engrossed as a child. Her hair was drawn back severely from her face, exposing the bone structure, with its profound assurance of beauty. His eyes flickered over her brilliant, inscrutable, a turbulent blue-green.

"Please stay with me. Please. I lost you." Her hand tightened on his and she gave the faintest moving smile, like all the lost youth in the world. She seemed a little delirious, this waif of disaster, as she tried to drag herself up. His hands shifted with exquisite strength to the fine bones of her shoulders, pressing her gently back into the pillows.

"It's all right, little one, I'm here. I won't go away. Lie still."

She subsided, solaced, her eyes glazing a little as though overlaid by a fine film.

"Hold my hand. Can you? Don't go away!" She seemed thankful to have an existence at all as long as their hands were joined and inseparable. He caught her agitated fingers with his own. His skin was as dark as a native's, lean and strong against her pale fragility. It was a curious sensation, almost a vast irrationality, having this child look at him with such trusting acceptance. Women didn't usually look at him with those eyes.

Her body was curved towards him, hovering delicately on the last edge of fragility, sighing in relief against the hard hand that held her. He clamped down on the thoughts that invaded his head.

"Tell me your name."

"Andrea, isn't it?" Her voice fell low, almost rambling. "My head aches, abominably." She shivered suddenly. "I'm ill."

"Do you know where you are, Andrea?" he persisted.

"In hospital. Does it matter?" Her voice was starting to slur and this prompted him to say with a gentleness not usual in him:

"No, it doesn't really matter at all. Lie quietly."

He changed his own position slightly after a close scrutiny of her face, the sinking eyelids.

Her voice surprised him, suddenly sharpening. "Don't go!"

"I've no such intention. I'm here and I'm staying!" His tone, curiously harsh, had the effect of soothing her. Her lashes tumbled on her shining porcelain cheeks.

Where the hell was Freedman? He didn't like this insidious drowsy state. His other hand found her pulse. It was very slow, wasn't it? The time had come for a second opinion. He knew enough about head injuries to expect almost anything. His mind shied away from the possible dangers. *He'd* taken enough to find her. She wasn't going to die on him now. Characteristically his face hardened to a granite impassivity. Steven Daintree was a man temperamentally unsuited to accepting defeat or failure.

He turned his dark head sharply as Luke Freedman appeared at the door, walking noiselessly on his rubber-soled shoes.

"Afternoon, Daintree. Sorry I got tied up. A hectic day all round."

Steven Daintree got to his feet, a lean, powerfully built man, his dark face undeniably autocratic, demanding some quick answers.

"Something tells me this girl is heading for trouble. That's your department. You'd better alert me. I want to be ready to meet it before it arrives!"

Immediately hostility was in the air, live and crackling with tension.

"Oh, come now!" Freedman tried to speak calmly, conscious of his own swift rise in blood pressure. "Her chart's been kept right up to the minute. She's holding her condition. Of course, if you're not satisfied..." he broke off, mortified and affronted.

"Oh, be your age, man!" Daintree bit off the words savagely. "Haul down the flag. A second opinion never hurt anyone!"

Luke Freedman reached for the pulse chart, grappling seriously with himself. Why should he allow Daintree to panic him? In all probability this would turn out to be a perfectly straightforward case. He couldn't afford to get his hackles up. It was Daintree, in a way, who had swung his appointment for him, over a much older man. There was nothing in the chart to alarm him, though it had been kept at two-hourly instead of hourly intervals. He leant over the bed.

"Andrea, how are you?"

He spoke loudly, almost in her ear, but she didn't react at all. He tried again and finally sank his fingers into the soft flesh of her upper arm.

"Andrea, wake up!"

She opened her eyes then with no real accommodation of the pupils. She frowned and refocused her gaze, passing from him to Daintree, who stood at his shoulder more like a mentor than a visitor, he thought with uncontrollable resentment, feeling very much on the defensive as he sometimes used to in his student days with a particular tutor.

There were footsteps along the corridor and Nurse Harris paused on the threshold, her round face sensitive to the charging tension, the grouping of the tableau, the air of constraint between the two men.

"How long has she been like this?" Doctor Freedman suddenly asked, his voice rising.

Over the pleasant round face spread a look of virtuous indignation.

"Well, really, Doctor, she's been quite all right. No trouble at all – quite lucid between sleeping bouts."

He took the inert wrist on the top sheet. The pulse was slow, much slower than the last entry. In fact it had been falling since late morning, combined with a rising temperature. Intracranial pressure now seemed likely. He swallowed dryly, an unpleasant diagnosis being forced home on him. He turned to the taller Daintree with the air of a man forced under fire to take orders from the enemy.

"She could need neuro-surgery, and soon. We haven't the facilities or the know-how."

A muscle moved along Daintree's lean cheek. "That I *know*. I was just waiting for you to confirm it." He lapsed into an abrupt silence as though to keep a restraint on his tongue.

Freedman nibbled savagely on his underlip. Haul down

the flag, he had said. Well, he'd have to. Daintree had all the connections, money to burn. Sturm was their man and he was pricey. *And* he was hundreds of miles away. He jerked irritably, his hands clasped together in a knuckle-whitening grip.

"The man I'd recommend is Guy Sturm of St. Vincent's. He has his department there, his own theatre, his own team – necessary for his kind of work. His fees are astronomical where the patient can afford them. Aside from that how do we get her there?"

Daintree made a sharp impatient sound. "Leave that to me. We'll have to fly her out, of course. You'll go with her?" He shot Freedman a piercingly bright glance from under his dark flaring brows.

"Of course. Could you arrange to fly me back? Morrison can take over in my absence."

"That can be arranged. I take it you'll contact Sturm while I line up the transport?"

Freedman nodded shortly. "Leave that part to me. I'll put in a priority call now. If there's bleeding going on inside her head, which now seems likely, an operation is inevitable. Twelve to fourteen hours at the most."

Daintree crossed to the door with spare, economical movements. "You can expect me to line up a charter flight within the hour. She'll want something bigger, more comfortable than what I can provide. Will you be ready to move?"

Freedman almost whistled. Within the hour! The race was about to start, but on it depended a girl's life. Daintree looked implacable, transfixing him with a brilliant stare. He glanced sideways at Nurse Harris who almost had her mouth open.

"That will do, Nurse," he said sharply. "You might send Matron to me." He looked past her stiffly retreating figure to Daintree. How in God's name had he come into all of this? The reins of authority were being taken right out of his hands. Something about Daintree would always give him the psychological advantage, that curious rather frightening detachment. Even when he looked at the girl there was no softening, no hint of compassion in that austerely handsome face. He knew to a hair's breath that Daintree had waited long enough for his answer.

"In an hour," he said curtly. "I'll be ready. Depend upon it. And Daintree . . ." he waited until the other man swung a brief lightning glance over his shoulder . . . "thank you!"

The blue-green eyes held a look that was hard to interpret. "Forget it," he said crisply. "We've both got a job to do!"

CHAPTER III

In the changing room he reached for the familiar things – the mask, the cap, and the gown. It was a privilege to be allowed to sit in on the operation – Sturm was very particular about whom he allowed into his theatre – yet somehow he was sick to the pit of his stomach. Familiar smells wafted in to him from the ante-room, reminding him this was a race against time. It was so unwise to become emotionally involved with a patient. It laid one open to self-exacerbation.

The door behind him opened and Guy Sturm walked in, very spare in the light, tight-fitting gear he wore under his gown. He was a tall man in fine physical condition with a silver halo of hair Freedman considered appropriate and bright, hard blue eyes. A forceful, rather temperamental man with the reputation of possessing a tongue as sharp and unerring as his scalpel. In his student days, Freedman had cause to circulate many stories of the great man's prowess in that direction, not always to Sturm's credit.

"All set, Freedman?" The voice was the acid drawl he remembered. "Not suffering from the nervous belly-aches, I hope. You always were lily-livered. Time is passing and a great deal to do. Patient's respiration rate is falling. A damn fool nurse out there was nearly blabbing her head off about cutting all that 'gorgeous' hair. A very silly young woman even as young women go. Can't expect too much of them, eh? They don't make all that much sense!"

Freedman returned the pebbled blue gaze and strove to

cover his helpless animosity. These brilliant, sarcastic types gave him a pain in the neck.

"Hopeless, the lot of them!" Sturm was saying, taking his silence for agreement. The mobile mouth curved down in his clever-ugly face. "Unobjective and sentimental. Barely a one worth talking to, I assure you. With all humbleness, I can't think how I ever married, except for my sons." His eyes fell on Freedman's set face. "Come in handy sometimes, eh, Freedman? As I expect you know."

Freedman lifted his head, obliged to return that grin for what it was worth. Who knew, the temperamental old devil might take it into his head to throw him out. No one could deny that Guy Sturm was a very able man, in fact no one had ever had the temerity to do such a thing, but Freedman was of the opinion that a little of the great man went a long way. To be taken a small dose only, like once a year. He reflected rather waspishly that Grace Sturm always referred to herself as "the duffer" for reasons one had scarcely to guess at.

They both turned as the door opened and Theatre Sister announced very briskly:

"All set, sir!"

Sturm produced a pair of glasses and poked them on the bridge of his nose.

"No need to yell, girl! This isn't a football match, is it?"

Theatre Sister stood her ground, answering bravely: "I wasn't aware that I *was* yelling, sir!"

"Bunkum!" said the great man rudely. He swerved and subjected Freedman to a close scrutiny as though he had only just noticed his existence. "You look a bit green, my boy. No call to be nervous. All things being equal I'll pull your little ewe lamb round in under the hour, wouldn't

36

you say, Sister? If a job's worth doing, it's worth doing well! "

With a smile on his face he prepared to walk out of the room, pausing as he passed Theatre Sister, respectfully backed against the door, to jab her with a long finger, bending on her a startlingly lascivious grin.

"What you need is more fun in your spare time, Sister," he suggested.

"You might be right, sir," she smiled slightly. "But I rather doubt it! " She was wearing a good-tempered common sense like a badge and Freedman gave her a second glance. She was attractive in a way; a calm, intelligent, young woman with curious greeny-brown eyes, but they couldn't compare with a clear, shining grey, he thought rather distractedly.

"What do you say, Freedman?" Sturm's eyes fell on him.

"I'm sorry, sir, I've rather lost the thread of what we were saying."

"It would appear so," Sturm replied coldly. "You're very jumpy, aren't you? Never made a surgeon, like I told you. No nerve at all."

"Quite, sir! " They fell into line behind him. "I dare say it's my fault."

"I agree! " Sturm threw a sour smile over his shoulder. "Well, come along. Let someone else take the responsibility—I'm in excellent form."

Theatre Sister threw Freedman a sympathetic smile and let her Chief get ahead of them.

"No false modesty about *him*! " she said lightly.

Freedman frowned moodily. "I'd say he was just about the most arrogant old prima donna I've ever come across! "

Her voice was suddenly cool and casual. "Well, we're

all in favour of him around here." She was once more part of the team, her loyalty asserting itself. "The nice, admirable things don't always go along with brilliance, you know."

"That may well be," he retorted mildly enough. "Who am I to expect uniformity?"

She glimpsed the weariness and anxiety in his eyes and her own eyes softened. "I can see you're worried, Doctor, but you know as well as I do she's in the best possible hands. Now let's go in."

His eyes were diverted to the narrow, sheeted oblong on the table. Not even a human outline could be detected. Scrubbed up, masked and gowned, Sturm approached the table. Inside the theatre his demeanour underwent a startling change. He was no longer the silver-haired prima donna but a big, clever man, supremely rational, with the fires of brilliance and dedication burning brightly out of his blue eyes, the beautiful hands that moved with incredible delicacy and precision.

Pressed back against the wall, well clear of those who had things to do, Freedman found himself in an almost oppressive stupor of nerves and inactivity. The anaesthetist, a friend from intern days, sat on his low stool at the side of the table, stethoscope to his ears, making tiny marks on his chart. All eyes were glued on Sturm's steady, precise hands. There was no sound at all except the voice of the surgeon at intervals and finally his long-drawn sigh as the thin steel encountered its objective, the blood clot it had been seeking. Around the theatre swept an inaudible ripple of relief and triumph. Matt Sanders, the anaesthetist, gave him a half wink.

The human being under the green twill cover, impervious to pain, suddenly came to life.

"Take the sheet off me! Take it off. I'm suffocating!"

A faint smile came into Sturm's blue eyes. "All in good time, my dear. Diathermy, Sister!"

The young voice wore on, sometimes clear, sometimes garbled – nothing that made much sense, more a helpless reaction to the condition she found herself in. Only once did she sob aloud when the inevitable pain came, the suturing of the scalp, and then Freedman found himself swallowing hard and convulsively, his nails dragging into his palms. Then it was over and they were lifting her with great gentleness and care from the table on to the bed that had been wheeled in.

Sturm stepped back from the table while Theatre Sister whipped off his mask. "She'll do!" he said with immense satisfaction. "Now I'll have a chat to our man, Daintree. Panic-proof, that one. You might take a few lessons from him, Doctor." Sturm could turn any conversation to correction, but Freedman ignored that obvious jibe. Why wouldn't Sturm admire Daintree? These hard, self-controlled men counted such things a virtue. They were stripped of their theatre gear within minutes and walking along the empty corridor to where Daintree was waiting, Sturm slightly ahead as befitting his position, Freedman a few paces behind, neither concealing their gratification.

Steven Daintree advanced on Sturm, one hand extended, force and quality stamped all over him, in the set of his head and shoulders, the strong structure of his face with its emphatic lines. Temperament and character Freedman was prepared to concede, but he still didn't like the man. Sturm obviously did, shaking the younger man's hand and warmly accepting his thanks and congratulations. Elated with his own success, he was moved to be generous.

"Freedman here did a good job on the diagnosis. It was

39

very well spotted."

Freedman, meeting Daintree's glinting, blue-green gaze, suddenly blushed.

"I made no contribution at all."

"Come now, Doctor," Sturm remonstrated, but was already motioning Daintree towards his office. Freedman excused himself briefly on the pretext of having a word with Matt Sanders before he left the hospital for his private rooms.

"Join us as soon as you can, my boy!" Sturm threw over his shoulder with pseudo-friendliness. "Interesting case! I'd like to discuss it further."

Freedman inclined his head no more than politely. He was no boot-licker, not yet anyway. Even so he had to smile, for his laudable stand was wasted on Sturm. Already the great man had turned back to Daintree to say amicably:

"I understand you brought her in, my dear chap. Tell me about it."

See how the big wheels love one another! Freedman thought with unaccustomed irony. Better Daintree than himself, Guy Sturm had the reputation for being able to talk the hind leg off a donkey. He walked away down the corridor, making a conscious effort to pull himself together. He was growing cynical, prone to disenchantment. For the past few days he hadn't been at all himself, more like a change of personality, so much so that he was forced back on himself, able to recognize clearly for the first time in himself a sneaking envy, a fear of being patronised by men of a bolder, more individual stamp than himself. The thought gave him a chilling discomfort which made him anxious to escape the big, impersonal hospital with its top-flight resident specialists, for his own home ground where he was known and respected for what he was: a capable, hard-working G.P. with no pretensions to brilliance like nine out of ten of his fellows. Pursuing the truth, one had to face up to it. He was run-of-the-mill, but in that estimate, like most sensitive people, he was hard on himself.

Matt Sanders was hanging about near the lifts, hands shoved deep in his pockets, just like the old days. They spent a pleasant ten minutes talking over old times; the interesting, the comfortable, the sometimes hilarious things that had happened to them, then in a better frame of mind, Freedman approached Ward Sister to ask where they had taken his patient.

He found the room easily, not going in, but standing outside the door looking through the porthole glass windows. She was lying quietly, her breathing easy, the composition of her face altered by its attendant bandages.

Poor little girl! Poor little Andrea! He almost framed the words aloud. She had come through a bad time of it and there was still a long way to go. With a certain wry humour he recalled Sturm's cold-blooded commentary on the cutting of her long, beautiful hair. Trust a man like Sturm to see through to essentials. Like the "fool nurse" he would probably have found himself, if not "blabbing", at least upset at such a work of destruction.

Ward Sister had followed him up, wondering at his hesitation outside the door. She was a warmly pretty woman in her early thirties with a straight, direct gaze that still managed to be gentle and compassionate.

"Anything wrong, Doctor?"

"No, Sister," he smiled slightly. "She looks so peaceful, I won't disturb her. I just thought I'd see how she was."

"I understand it was a fine job Mr. Sturm did on her?" she prompted him gently.

41

"Quite in keeping with his reputation," he agreed without surprise and a certain lack of reverence.

She allowed herself to smile outright. She had grown used to Guy Sturm as a controversial subject. The eminent surgeon collected enemies like some men made friends.

"Theatre Sister had the good idea of making a switch of Miss Swanson's hair," she supplied, adroitly changing the subject. "We thought she could have it made up into a short wig until her own hair grows through. That colour would be almost impossible to duplicate in any case." A smile hovered around her mouth, reached her eyes. "Appearances are important to us girls, Doctor!"

His lingering resentment disappeared with that unexpected information.

"Of course, what a good idea!" he said rather artlessly. "I'd never have thought of it myself."

"That figures, Doctor," she smiled at this masculine revelation, her eyes lighting up with amusement. He suddenly found himself laughing and she offered quite genuinely:

"As a matter of fact, I could attend to it myself. The lass that lives next door to me runs her own hairdressing salon. She's bound to know the best person to handle the job. I'd be pleased to do it after all that child's been through."

"That's very kind of you, Sister," he said quietly. "I'm sure she'll be most grateful."

"No trouble at all, Doctor." She was watching his face rather quizzically and he turned his profile with the disquieting sense that she realised, intuitively, that his interest was more than professional. He allowed himself only one more glance through the small circular window at that calm, pale face. It was entirely colourless beneath its

42

bandages except for the thick dark lashes that lay like spread fans on her cheeks. One thing was certain, their paths would cross again, even if he had to move mountains to effect it!

Summer was running out fast. The banks of hydrangeas that ran the full length of the hospital gardens were turning from their dense blue and pink to a speckled rust and the last of the lavender blue bells of the jacarandas had fallen.

Andrea lay back in her deck-chair on the side veranda letting the afternoon breeze play through the newly emerged, shining, silky soft tendrils and lovelocks that clung to her scalp and bordered her fine, high forehead like a very small child's. It was a gentle breeze and she was as fragile and frail as a butterfly outspread in the sunshine. In another ten days she was due for discharge. What then? Her progress had been slow, much slower than had been anticipated, but this was attributed to a combination of factors that had piled up against her.

For the past week she had been feeling stronger in herself, but all the other summers of her life prior to her accident had gone into oblivion. The driving longing of the early days of recovery had been replaced by a quietly desperate resignation, though sometimes, in dreams, her suppressed subconscious gained on her, playing tricks of total unreality, fragments and visions that must have come from another life, closing over her head like floodwater. These were the nightmares, but Night Sister was always there, a hand on her shoulder, a soothing, matter-of-fact voice: "Andrea, wake up!" bringing her out of it. At those times, Night Sister was Andrea's favourite woman in the whole wide world.

Sunlight fell in a warm, golden glow across her shut

eyelids. Steven promised to come today – something to grip hard on for a person without direction. It was only the third visit in many long weeks, but that seemed momentarily irrelevant. He was a busy man and Mokhana was hundreds of miles away. Beneath her quiet gentleness a slow excitement was gathering. He pulled her in such a strange way. She had only to think of him ... for she remembered exactly each detail of his appearance.

Abruptly she sat forward and looked down at her wrists, more fragile than ever, but the broken bones had healed. She would have to school herself to careful composure, but the thought of seeing him set up some physical compulsion impossible to control. Perhaps it was nerves that made the strong young pump of her heart seem faster? There was a soft footfall behind her and she turned her face expectantly over her shoulder, her large grey eyes crystal clear.

It wasn't Steven, but a woman. A woman, moreover, of her own physical type – blonde and slender, light-eyed, with superlative skin. Almost a fragile person, small-boned, small-hipped, her legs long and smooth; an elegant, expensively dressed woman with pale hair wrapped around her head like a ballet dancer. Andrea put her age at about thirty-eight, when in fact she was considerably older. Unaccountably she felt her nape prickle and her eyes went blank. God, was this hellish period of forgetfulness ever to end? Did she know this woman looking at her so expectantly?

"Andrea!" the woman said, confirming her fears. Her face betrayed her apprehension and she gripped the sides of her chair tightly. Her mouth felt as though it had dried up and tension was mounting in her until it was a bewildering pain.

"Yes?"

The pale blue eyes were roaming all over her head, taking stock of the ash-blonde tendrils as short and silky as swansdown, making her feel extremely self-conscious in a way no one had ever done even at the beginning. There was a curious glint of suppressed excitement about those eyes that shifted to probe the contours of her face so piquantly at odds with the "small boy" hair. She was searching for something, but for what? There was a desolate, lonesome look to the pale blue depths like cold water breaking against rocks.

"Irina Godden!" the woman introduced herself at last, rather jerkily for someone of her expected poise. "I'm sorry I startled you, my dear. Were you expecting someone?" One hand fluttered to the corridor beyond them, as smooth and silkily preserved as only that of a wealthy woman with household staff could be.

An incredibly swift play of emotion crossed Andrea's face, then it was composed again, grave and remote like a painting. "Mrs. Godden, of course!" The pilot's name had been Godden. Perhaps this was his wife?

"Please sit down!" She shifted her own position slightly, indicating the chair beside her with a gesture of friendship that was more than mere greeting. The woman took it with a certain tension, a shock-absorber tautness to the long line of her back. She was unable to relax in the warm, scented ambience of that golden afternoon and Andrea knew by instinct that she was deeply upset and would in turn inflict her own kind of chaos. The pale eyes were holding hers with intensity, almost it could be believed, on the verge of tears.

"I'm glad we can talk at last, my dear," she said huskily. "I've no intention of rocking the boat, if that's what they're afraid of, and I've been ill myself. There are just

45

so many things I must know." Her voice cracked, strangely bitter, making Andrea feel uneasiness and pity all mingled at once. She found her voice impulsively.

"Please allow me to say how deeply sorry I am, Mrs. Godden. I know how you must be feeling!"

"Sorry!" The pale head jerked up almost fiercely and Andrea had difficulty not recoiling. It was that kind of a response she couldn't have been mistaken. The pale eyes narrowed. "That's a strange word to choose when you're speaking of Carl . . . my son!"

"Your son?" That harsh outcry had made Andrea's heart jump. Her whole body seemed to flicker. "I'm sorry, I had no idea. I thought perhaps it might have been your husband."

For a moment Irina Godden looked almost bewildered, quite genuinely shocked, then her brows drew together and her pale eyes glinted startlingly sinister. "What *is* this, my dear? You're quite rational, aren't you?"

"I hope so!" Andrea heard her own voice, slightly wry but shaking a little. She could search and recall and probe in vain. There was nothing. "I'm sorry, Mrs. Godden," she said again, then added by way of explanation, "You don't know, obviously. I can't remember anything that happened to me before the accident. Nothing. Not my father, my life or my friends. Not even your son. I'm so very sorry. It's inadequate, I know, but the best word I can think of."

Irina Godden jerked off one of her rings and thrust it back on her finger, almost blinded by the incipient blue fire.

"Good God!" she said tonelessly. "Why wasn't I told?"

Andrea turned her head. "Is it important?"

The older woman sighed deeply. "My deerest child, of

course it's important. You were *engaged* to my son, the fiancée he was bringing home. All I have left."

Andrea stared back at her until the pupils of her eyes had dilated, encroaching on the irises shining like sovereigns. "No!"

"Can't you remember at all?" Irina Godden persisted fiercely.

"No!" It had to be said. No! No! she wanted to scream her denials to the whole world. Her head was beginning to thump with a tension headaches as bad as they had ever been.

Irina Godden's light eyes glittered. She bent forward a little, her lips parted. She seemed almost breathless. Andrea found she couldn't withstand that avid gaze. She fixed her own eyes on the scarlet poppies in the garden, dancing in a shimmering haze.

"So this is what they've been keeping from me," the older woman said bitterly. "Putting me off endlessly, endlessly. But not any more!" Her head swung back with a certain purpose. "You need taking care of, my child, but you have youth on your side. Youth is resilient. Amnesia doesn't kill, it's a strictly temporary disability. I may have lost a son, but the girl he loved has been spared to me – a beautiful girl, as I might have known. Carl inherited his aesthetic sense from me."

Andrea felt the trembling shock of it right through her nervous system. She lay back in her chair, hopelessly defeated. What more was there to uncover? A fiancée? Her body was a traitor, for she felt she had never been in love in her life. Never been stirred by a man, until . . . She sighed painfully. This woman would never understand. For the first time she appeared to relax. Irina Godden began to talk, slowly and softly at first, then gathering momentum with frightening speed.

She spoke of Carl's childhood, proud and happy recollection. Carl had always been special. Carl as a student, careless and clever, Carl as a young man; all the girls who had loved him, not a one of them good enough; the dreams that they both had cherished, dreams that were forever jettisoned. It hurt so to go back over the past, but she must! Her voice droned on, self-sufficient unto itself. She was oblivious to Andrea's funny little moan of blind frustration. But she was too far gone to have heeded it even if she had.

Andrea sat there wanting to cry, a burning pain in her chest. She looked trapped and at bay like a small wild creature, yet she was determined she wouldn't cry. Her eyes remained fixed on that point in the garden, a vivid spray of hope. Always at the back of her mind she nurtured the belief that she would remember everything all at once. It would all come back to her, miraculously.

"Carl?" she whispered the name aloud painfully, hopefully, clutching at straws in the wind.

Irina grasped her shoulder, the long fingers biting in, her eyes lighting with incredulous joy. "You remember!"

Andrea forced herself to meet those strange eyes. A needle of pain struck into her chest. "No. I'm sorry. I hope and hope. Wishing and longing, and always this total blank."

The fingers tightened on her shoulder. "You're not lying to me, are you, for some reason? Girls have been known to lie before this. Believe me, I'll find out!"

Andrea sat there, stunned by the look on the woman's face, the hard voice compressed and dry. Her mind searched frantically, aimlessly, for something that might mean something to this woman. She hadn't felt anything like this before, yet she understood with horror what this woman might be feeling.

"Answer me!" Irina Godden suddenly shook her hard so that her head snapped back on her slender neck.

"Mrs. Godden!" The voice was icy, cutting across the shocked silence like a knife, causing Irina Godden to turn in sudden alarm. She jumped to her feet, her face severe, tight with anticipation of trouble, for she had awaited her opportunity coming along the veranda without permission, entirely unannounced. Another woman she might have subdued with the force of her husband's wealth and social standing, but Steven Daintree was beyond her control, arrogant and supremely sure of himself, just like his father had been.

He loomed tall and strikingly handsome in the doorway, giving the oddest impression of some powerful black panther coiled to strike. Irina Godden gave a quiver of fright, losing control of the situation, shaking her head with a small gasp.

"You startled me, Mr. Daintree!"

She looked more than startled, Andrea thought catching a shade of the woman's fright. He *did* look so terribly formidable, yet her throat was rippling with a crazy kind of relief, for now the short nightmare was over. Irina Godden was standing her ground looking appalled to her very roots, but Andrea was free of that fixated stare.

"That was obvious!" he returned curtly, his brilliant blue-green gaze moving over Andrea. "Are you all right?"

She nodded her head without speaking, but it was all there in her face; the dangerous frailty, fear, astonishment, a dreadful uncertainty. The warm scented air brushed her face and she put up a hand to find her cheeks burning hot.

"You might have at least told me she was suffering from loss of memory!" Irina Godden hurled at him, her voice accusing, firming to aggression, as she made a desperate effort to wrench the advantage from him.

He was entirely unmoved by her outburst, betraying none of his own feelings beyond a superficial scrutiny of her face.

"My dear Mrs. Godden, it wasn't my place to relay Andrea's medical condition. Her doctors considered it inadvisable to confront her with too many issues at once. Her physical progress has been slow enough, God knows. You might have realised this. I take it you've put her completely in the picture!"

"I have!" Tiny points of triumph flared in her eyes.

His mouth thinned. "On reflection do you consider that was wise?" He pressed the point swiftly. "You might take the time to look at her properly – the eyes mostly. A hunted doe might be evocative."

She ran her tongue along her lips to gain precious seconds. Some sub-stratum of her mind was conscious of those enormous troubled eyes, the curious fragility. Because of it she over-defended herself, passionately, angrily.

"I'm here by design, Mr. Daintree, not by accident."

"And quite without permission!" He cut the ground from under her feet.

She flushed alarmingly. "Had I need of an excuse I want only to take Andrea home with me whenever she's ready. My only wish is to make things up to her!"

Smother her, more likely, he thought with ironic perception. Judging by her brittle, strung-up manner Irina Godden was heading for some kind of breakdown. The girl might at least be spared that. Out of the corner of his eyes he could see she had gone rigidly still, lying back in her deckchair and looking fragile enough to be breakable.

He gave a brief smile, attractive and calculating.

"That is very kind of you, Mrs. Godden, and I'm sure Andrea appreciates your thoughtfulness and generosity, but the fact is she's already accepted my aunt's invitation to convalesce on Mokhana."

They were looking hard at each other – he, superbly composed with a sort of vibrancy about him, eyes brilliant like a discharge of electricity, she, flushed yet dangerous, a woman unequal to withstanding rebuffs of any kind.

"So another little problem is solved, is it?" she asked, her voice suddenly dripping saccharine. "It's common knowledge that invitations to Mokhana are few and far between since your mother's day, unless it's a senator or a visiting dignitary or whatever. You're very cavalier all of a sudden!"

"Any objection?" he asked positively.

"Every objection, Mr. Daintree. How do you imagine you can get me to agree to this?"

"By appealing to your better nature, perhaps," he smiled without amusement. "To be honest, Mrs. Godden, I didn't realise your permission was in any way relevant. It may well be that Andrea might wish to visit you some time in the future, but for now ... let's say she's committed to convalescing on Mokhana. As a matter of interest I've just been discussing it with Guy Sturm."

"Don't try me, Mr. Daintree," she said with barely controlled fury. That dark handsome face with its trace of coldness and disdain was one she would dearly have liked to hit out at because it made her feel stupid and weak; a foolish, excitable woman.

His mouth was touched with satire. "*Try* you! That was hardly my intention!" He swung his imperious dark head towards the girl. "Andrea?"

She knew exactly what she had to say as clearly as if

he had handed her a set of instructions. Her face was white and strained and she spoke her words as if she had just learnt them.

"It was kind of you to think of me, Mrs. Godden, and I do appreciate it, but it's as Steven told you, I've accepted his invitation to visit Mokhana."

"*Steven?*" Irina Godden grabbed at the operative word. Her fine light brown eyebrows shot upwards and she gave a tinkle of laughter, delicately insinuating and very unpleasant.

"You're making a mistake, my dear, a bad one. But I still have a week or so to prove it to you. I want you to understand, Andrea, you have an obligation to me as Carl's mother. He would have wanted you to come home with me, be part of the family now you have none of your own. I need your comfort. You're beautiful and a lady. You would fit in well. Try thinking about it and you'll know I'm right. There are things I must know about my son's last months, last days, last moments. It's tearing my heart out. Can't you understand?"

"Of course I can!" Andrea shivered, unable to penetrate the recesses of her own mind but able quite clearly to see this woman's dilemma. "Please don't distress yourself, Mrs. Godden, but you must see I can't help you however much I want to. I can't even help myself. Please be patient. As soon as I can remember anything at all about . . . about . . . Carl," she stumbled, and hurried on, "I'll tell you, I promise!"

Irina Godden seemed wholly consumed by anguish. "But when? When? When will that be?" The evidence was there in her working mouth, the over-bright eyes.

"Obviously she can't say," Steven Daintree said bluntly.

A blind resentment took hold of her mind. "*He's* not

your answer!" she said harshly, not understanding her fear of him, unless it was his height and strength, that dark vitality.

"I owe him my life!" the girl said quietly.

"You owe him nothing!"

Steven Daintree broke in again. "I agree!" he said smoothly, using one of his dominating gestures arousing anger without effort for his own ends. "Nevertheless she will be accepting my hospitality."

Irina felt a shoot of anger rip through her. "We'll see, Mr. Daintree." She pushed her chair awkwardly aside. "I have a few cards of my own to play, ones you don't know about." There was a small hesitation and her eyes moved to Andrea. "I'll be back with my husband. He's very like Carl, you know. We'll take you away and get you well soon." She suddenly looked her age, tired and distraught. "I can see why my son loved you. You reminded him of me. I was a beauty too, at your age." Her voice froze with dislike. "Good day, Mr. Daintree, I suppose you have a system of your own that you adhere to?"

"I do, and it works, Mrs. Godden," he replied suavely. She tilted her fair head in a savage but unconscious gesture of resignation and swept away along the veranda, leaving the lingering faint trace of her expensive perfume.

"Spare me women!" Steven murmured laconically. "Alluring as impressions, but God help you when you're confronted with the details!"

Her eyes slipped over the hard planes of his face. "That's rather cruel, Steven!"

"But I *am* cruel, little one. Didn't you know?"

The frail cord of tension snapped between them. She smiled with her eyes. "I don't think so!"

Abruptly he beat a soundless little rhythm on the back

53

of the chair, then lowered himself into it. "You're a babe – a babe found in a rain forest!"

"Perhaps, but I feel sorry for that woman all the same."

The face that regarded her was no longer impersonal. There was a hint of anger in those brilliant, ever changing eyes. "You'd feel a lot sorrier for yourself if I allowed her to gobble you up." His eyes pinned her to the chair. "Do you want to fall in with her plan?"

"You know I don't!" She bent her shining head.

"Well then!"

Something caused her to plough on. She turned her face along the chair and studied that dark, imperious profile.

"Perhaps she was right and I do have a responsibility to her because of . . . because . . ."

He jerked his chair back and got up, towering over her. She followed the line of his powerful shoulders with her eyes.

"My dear child, grow up!" he said forcibly. "Irina Godden has gone through life recognising no other rights but her own. At best she's a chronic seeker of her own self-interests. In a few months' time when you're more her weight you can tackle her again. *If* you still want to!" He allowed himself to look back at her. The pale skin was flawless, translucent like alabaster, but the fine bone structure was too near the skin. There were hollows under her cheekbones; in her delicate throat. He made a rapid gesture, almost of irritation, and she looked up at him with her shadowed tip-tilted eyes.

"Were you really discussing me with Mr. Sturm?"

He smiled slightly. "No, as a matter of fact I just missed him. It was his second in command I was speaking to."

"So it was a lie, then?"

It was difficult to tell, but she fancied she saw his mouth soften.

"Don't work yourself up into anything, little one. In ten days' time I'm taking you back to Mokhana. You don't have to do a thing but put some flesh on those bones and grow out your hair."

She felt troubled by that lightning glance but managed not to put up a hand to her head. "Is it so very terrible?"

He returned her gaze very coolly, composed and sleek.

"Terrible? No. It's rather touching and unexpected and a damned good defence."

"I don't understand you!"

"Of course you don't!" He narrowed his eyes and she murmured in confusion:

"Oh, Steven!"

"What's wrong? It was an innocent enough remark. Could mean almost anything." His eyes flicked over her face. "How you ever got mixed up with young Godden I'll never know!"

She shook her head. "Don't *say* that! I'm the one who might never know. At least that would be nearer the truth."

He leant back against the rail, hard and lean, the beautiful cloth of his jacket sheened by the sun. "Don't worry, little one," he said consolingly. "It will all come back, though I don't give a damn if you never remember."

"Steven!" She felt a shock of pain tilting her head to look up at him. She could almost feel his features tauten.

"Why shouldn't your life begin in a rain forest? It's as good a place as any to be re-born."

"You talk in riddles," she said plaintively, looking away from the merciless gleam in his eyes. "Tell me about

55

Mokhana, your aunt. Will she really want me there?"

He gave a trace of a smile, coming back to sit beside her. "First of all, Andrea, Mokhana belongs to me. The invitation from my aunt was by way of camouflage, though she'll be pleased to welcome any guest of mine. Mokhana has been my aunt's home for very many years now. She is my father's only sister, and she was as devoted to him as she now is to me."

She traced the tips of her fingers over her chair. "She never married?"

"No, though she might have done any number of times. She's still a handsome woman and well into her fifties."

"And Mokhana?" she prompted gently.

"Mokhana, my child, is the pattern of my life!" He looked at her sidelong and she wondered that his voice could be so caressing. He smiled slightly and looked ahead again. "I have a feeling of strangeness almost any place else. It's the familiar and the beautiful. It's mine and I'm tied to it as surely as with a chain. Do you understand a man's need for possession, little faun?"

"I think I do!"

He didn't appear to agree. He reached for a cigarette and lit it, smoking quietly beside her, his brilliant eyes half closed like a cat's. "In the mornings you look out at the indigo line of the ranges. By afternoon they're smoky blue, lost in a heat haze. There are waterholes everywhere sheeted with lotus lilies, swamps and billabongs, lakes and lagoons as clear as your eyes. The bird life is fantastic; black swans, pelicans, herons and terns, black and white ibis, cranes, wild duck and magpie geese in the millions. I've even seen the grey, scarlet-capped brolgas stalking the lines of grazing cattle."

"*Mokhana!* It sounds beautiful," she said, seeing it through his eyes.

"Aboriginal, of course. A place where the brolga dances." He eased his long length back into the chair, his skin very dark against the frosty line of his collar. "My father bought the original selection with the gold his father left him from a fairly rich strike at Charters Towers. That was in the early days before he was married. One has to offer a decent home to a bride." His voice seemed to undergo some curious change, but he continued without further comment. "I've added to the property, made a lot of improvements to the house and the run that could never have been attempted before. It has character. I think you'll like it, but probably the grounds best of all. On Mokhana we have every kind of ornamental tree you can think of — an avenue of poincianas that people come miles to see, African tulip trees, tamarind, most of the tropical palms, cassias, great fig and mango trees, frangipani, hibiscus and bougainvillea, of course. The halvillia with its long golden flowers, scores of bauhinias and a jacaranda in front of the house."

"Your mother had a hand in it, it seems?"

"She did. She was interested enough at the beginning."

"Did she die, Steven?" she asked tentatively.

In the polished teak of his face his eyes were quite startling. "You got there in no time," he said a little brutally. "No, little one, she didn't die. She just cleared off and left us when I was about eleven. She's made another life for herself. She's a sculptress of some merit, I understand."

"I see," she said quietly.

"You don't see at all. How could you?" he said abruptly.

"Tell me some more about Mokhana," she pleaded with him, her eyes huge and intense. "You're different then."

"Am I?" Something appeared to amuse him, for his expression lightened. "All right then, anything to keep that look out of your eyes. For a long time now I've been experimenting with new types of pastures and grazing methods. They've paid off, fortunately for me and the industry. We run a lot of Zebus, Brahmans, Santa Gertrudis up north. British breeds don't do so well in the tropics, not in the heavy rainfall regions, and we're inundated in the Wet. This year I expect to spend a lot of money clearing the rain forest along my north-eastern border. It'll take a lot of capital, but it will be worth it in the long run." He turned to look at her. "Want to hear any more?"

She moistened her mouth with the tip of her tongue. "Of course!"

"Even you have tricks, little witch! Conscious or unconscious?"

"I'm only interested, Steven!"

Something in the quality of his expression made her heart leap in her breast. He seemed about to say something hurtful, but stopped, his smile hard and provoking:

"One should never lose sight of the red light," he said cryptically, then relaxed again. "From your recollections of the rain forest you'll know the North is quite different from the rest of the continent. The Tropic of Capricorn changes everything. The whole landscape changes. You're slap bang in the midst of lushness and brilliance, a flowering wilderness – the sea, and the jungle, the canefields as far as the eye can see, the cattle lands that spread back from the ranges through the Gulf to the Territory, the teeming wild-life, crocodile-infested rivers. Even the Reef, the Grand Canal, is only a stone's throw away by our lights."

The Reef! Something slipped through her mind and

out again like a faraway beam from a lighthouse. "The Barrier Reef?" she said strangely.

He turned to look at her, his eyes narrowing over her. "Yes, the Barrier Reef, Andrea. A continuous coral rampart running almost the distance from London to Leningrad."

"Yes, of course." She was shaking her head rather helplessly.

His voice was quite matter-of-fact. "You'll see it again even if you've seen it before – one of the great natural wonders of the world. In fact, if we can steer clear of the Godden clan I'll take you on a tour through the canefields, hundreds of miles when your immediate world is bounded by high walls of rich green cane, a cobalt sky and the red ochre earth. You might even see a canefield fired by night. If you do it's a spectacle you're not likely to forget, and everywhere in the air the heavy sweet smell of molasses." Somehow he seemed to infuse a world of excitement and expectation into his voice, for her alone.

"Why are you doing this for me, Steven?" she interrupted a little desperately.

He turned his head, his dark face saturnine. "I don't sit around analysing my motives, little one. I just *do* things. I leave all the rest to you women. You seem to love all the soul-searching, the whys and the wherefores. Thrive on it!"

To her horror she felt her eyelids brimming. Frantically she swallowed on the salt taste of them, but a tear splashed on to her cheek.

"Damn, damn!" She went to put up a hand, but he beat her to it and brushed away the tear with the tips of his fingers.

"You poor little scrap. I'm sorry! Now you've made me feel a miserable beast!"

She smiled at the inflection in his voice as he meant her to, but she took a long time before replying, still quivering from the touch of his hand. Then quite simply she said:

"You're very good to me, Steven."

"You're not afraid of words, then?" The old irony was back in his voice again, unexpectedly devastating.

"Are *you*?" she asked, surprising herself.

"Perhaps I won't always treat you gently," he evaded the question. "Have you thought of that?"

She coloured, her breathing urgent and deeper, but he had turned his head. "Oh, what the devil! Let's talk of something else!" He began reminiscing with odd bits and pieces, snatches of sardonic humour that made her want to laugh and cry at the same time. The afternoon wore on with a quality of bliss, yet unerringly she knew this was only an interlude. Perhaps it was true what they said; if someone saved your life you were in their debt for evermore. She only knew with a great certainty that always and for ever she would carry the memory of that moment in the jungle when she opened her eyes and looked up at him and knew herself safe.

CHAPTER IV

TEN days later Andrea flew into the startlingly beautiful sunset of the tropics, looking down at Mokhana for the first time. It spread out in a great curve inland from the rugged line of the ranges; grape-blue, densely forested, rearing dramatically against the sky of crimson and gold. Great flights of wild geese flew beneath them, winging on towards their homes in the swamps and the verdant, bush willow-hung billabongs. On their eastern border lay the rain forest with its narrow, boulder-choked chasms, all but impenetrable with its forest giants, lawyer vines, tree ferns and tangled undergrowth; its ancient cages of rock drawings, the legacy of some primitive tribe. Seen from the sky it was an awesome sight and Andrea shivered involuntarily, marvelling that she had ever come out of it alive.

From the moment Steven's lean, strong hands had encircled her narrow rib cage and lifted her into his pristine white, red and gold striped Piper Comanche she had felt no fear, no dread of reliving a nightmare, only a curious calm sense of homecoming. Beneath them thousands of head of Mokhana stock grazed on the rich loamy flats and everywhere was the circular silver glitter of lakes and lagoons the metallic threads of waterways that criss-crossed the run: beautiful, mysterious places, where the brolga danced its secret, ritual ballet, and the pelican built her nest.

They had flown over a thousand miles along the coast, coming in over the islands of jade, that threaded the purplish-pink rampants of coral, plunging a hundred fathoms to the ocean bed. It was indescribably beautiful, the gemstone facets of the sea, aqua, emerald and turquoise, almond green shallows, the ruffle of surf and the blindingly white boomerang beaches of the coral atolls — an experience so lyrical in quality that for once Andrea put the past out of her mind. She was beyond heartache, beyond pain. Only excitement was as keen as a razor's edge.

The hinterland was a checkerboard of luminously green canefields and richly red freshly ploughed fields, of pineapple plantations and pawpaw groves, of majestic acres of mango trees. They flew over the dairylands and on to the land of the beef cattle and the crocodile. Mokhana, Steven's home! It was like looking down at some small isolated settlement nestling in the valley. The homestead was set back on a crest surrounded by the home gardens and on their perimeter several much smaller buildings.

The landing strip ran out, a length of red ribbon before them, quite a few miles from the first of the outlying buildings. Then they were coming in! Only once as they were losing altitude coming down quickly in a brisk cross wind did Andrea know a terrible moment of fear; fear that held her in thrall until Steven's voice, hard to the point of curtness, brought her right out of it.

"Relax, child! Nothing in this wide world is going to hurt you!"

She stopped her convulsive swallowing and lay back in her seat with her eyes closed, not even opening them when the wheels touched down with a slight shudder and the speed of the aircraft slackened off abruptly until finally the engines cut and the deep shadows of the hangar fell across her eyelids. She heard his voice faintly amused, a little impatient:

"You can open your eyes now, little one. We're on the ground!"

"I'm nervous!" she said involuntarily. Her eyes were a soft, cloud grey, smiling but still faintly troubled.

"There's no need to be!" he said briefly, his mouth touched with the ghost of a smile, "unless it's of me!"

He got up and opened out the door of the plane, swinging lightly to the ground and holding up his hands for her. She didn't mean to tremble, but she did, her breathing suddenly difficult. She slipped quickly away from him and walked out into the daylight. Clouds rose in a sweep of fire across the horizon, tipping the tall tops of the trees, sunset red and gold, flaming wherever you looked. It was lush, vital country, thickly grassed with sweet, fattening herbage and grasses in a vivid shade of green.

The air was warm with a special clarity, bright-hued parrots wheeled overhead and a butcher bird called from the shady paperbarks that lined the strip. Andrea's eyes were drawn to a cinnamon-coloured station wagon with a cream top parked in the shade of a carport that adjoined the hangar. Bougainvillea climbed like a brilliant parasite all over its sides and roof and spilled on to the hangar, trailing heavy drifts of mauve and crimson blossom. Steven looked down at her small, entranced face.

"Go and sit in the car, it's not locked. I'll get your gear out."

She smiled at him and walked away, moving like a dancer, her body held high up in the small of her back, wondering how on earth she would ever have managed without him, for it had been Steven who, weeks ago, had gone to her small flat, paid off the balance of her rent and collected all of her worldly possessions that somehow, pathetically, seemed to fit into four brand-new suitcases. He had even found time to call on the headmistress of her former school and had quite a conversation with her, none of which he relayed to Andrea beyond a letter of sympathy and comfort from the staff and a huge sheaf of flowers signed by a whole list of unknown identities. Only a latent sense of humour saved her from breaking down and crying.

For weeks now, Steven had been the colour and shape of her existence. Stripped of everything, with nothing to remember, nothing to cling to, she only half realised her utter dependence on him. She opened the door of the car and slipped into the seat, more tired than she cared to admit. She wound down her window, then leaned across to do the same on the driver's side. The evening breeze was a soothing balm on her temples. She rested her head against the deep upholstery, content to wait for Steven.

He didn't take long, loading her cases into the back of the station wagon. Then he came around to the driver's side and settled his long length into the vehicle beside her. He looked about him for a moment, then leant across her to the glovebox to search out the keys. Briefly his eyes slipped over the soft, rather melancholy beauty of her face. If it hadn't been for the imperious cut of his mouth she might have thought there was a certain tenderness in his glance. But it wasn't tenderness and she didn't know what it was.

They went like the wind. His dark profile was without expression, remote even, with all the chiselled splendour of a head on a coin. Great spherical clumps of pampas grass waved silver-grey spears in greeting and a lagoon flashed by, a shimmering vision, floating beautiful violet-blue waterlilies. The warm, scented breeze and the speed of the vehicle were combining to act as an opiate on her. Her eyelids were heavy, drooping, despite all her efforts to absorb her surroundings. She let them fall for a brief respite and her face took on the quality of a soft dream.

About a mile from the house he pulled over on to the grassy verge and cut the engine. He remained still for a moment behind the wheel, his glance on her quiet face, then in a dark undertone he said her name:

"Andrea!"

The breeze from the open window had fluffed out the short silky strands of her hair until it formed a shining aura around her small proud head. The last rays of the sun, glinting through the window, lay in a gold bar across her delicate throat. He repeated her name and she awakened at once, her head lifting swiftly, the colour of her eyes intensifying. She met his gaze and colour crept under her skin making it less porcelain-like, warmer.

"I'm sorry, I must have drifted off."

His mouth twisted in amused exasperation. "You're utterly fantastic, child!"

"Oh . . . how is that?"

"You don't awaken like most people – with languor, sleepy-eyed. More like a doe in a forest ready to spring up and away at the slightest sound. Fully awake, head raised warily, wide, alert eyes!"

"I suppose it's true, if you say so!" From the tranquillity of her expression she was in no way disturbed by his comment. Her smile deepened, slowly, irresistibly.

Into his eyes came an odd expression. She looked back at him, suddenly helpless as though she was being pitched head first into a bottomless snowdrift. She wasn't in any way hurt, but she was trembling.

"Steven?" her voice had some faint melody running through it. "Why do you look at me like that?"

"Why should I not?" He looked down his straight nose at her. "This is my land and you're my . . , responsibility!"

"I'm sorry!"

"Being sorry has nothing to do with it," he said smoothly. "That's just the way it is. I knew almost from the first second I laid eyes on you I'd have you on my hands."

She looked away across the open savannahs, feigning interest in the dappled leaf patterns. "I could have made other arrangements, I suppose."

"You could have made nothing of the kind, and don't think I don't know about Nick Godden's visit!" He touched her cheek with a hard finger, turning her head back to him. "Whether we like it or not, we're linked together for a time. You're going to get well and strong on Mokhana and I'm going to see to it."

She tilted her chin up and away from him with her first show of spirit.

"I'm not an infant, Steven, to be cosseted and manipulated this way and that . . . be a good child and I'll buy you an ice-cream . . . I'm a woman!"

"What rot!" He laughed outright with a mixture of deep cynicism and a certain wry amusement. "You're half girl-child, half witch I brought out of the forest."

"Thank you, Mr. Daintree!" She showed him the tender exposed nape of her neck. "My hair *will* grow out again, you know!"

"How fascinating, but I wouldn't try and speed up the process if I were you!" There was a mysterious, untameable something to the depths of his eyes, a turbulent sea-change. She was a little afraid of those eyes. The thought entered her brain and went on and on. She moved her shoulders fretfully in some bewilderment, feeling shatteringly aware of him. There was a cool sensuality to his face she had never noticed before. Or maybe it was the quality of light of his mood. He changed so rapidly.

"You're not being very helpful!" she managed at last.

He gave a brief laugh. "I guess I wasn't trying! You know, Andrea, nothing ever turns out quite the way we plan, though some moments do have the power to change our lives. This memory loss of yours won't last for ever. Things will come back, bit by bit or all at once. I'm only a thread in the overall pattern."

"A gleaming one!" she said as the thought swept her.

There was a faint violence in the way he turned on her and her eyes went huge.

"You persist in seeing me as someone I'm *not*, cast in the heroic mould. I'm no knight in shining armour, little one. I can be damnable at times. Remember it. *And* this! Play it easily in the next few months, content to take things as they come. Don't be tempted to tire yourself out prematurely. Keep a brake on all those youthful emotions, and I can tell by your eyes and your mouth you have more than your share of them." He subjected her to a long scrutiny. "Will you remember, I wonder?"

"Do you expect me to forget?" she asked softly.

"I expect nothing from any woman!"

"No, I can see that!"

His head was turned away from her, upflung, dark and arrogant. It was an intensely male face, hard and alert, very self-contained. Yes, Steven could be a damnable man, she was forced to concede, yet a flicker of humour touched her mouth.

"I apologise for seeing some good in you, Mr. Daintree," she said silkily. "Knowing what *I* don't, *you* have every right to chastise me!"

Softly he turned on her. "You contrary little wretch!"

"You can't have it both ways." Her eyes were dancing in her pale, oval face. "You're heartless, Steven, *and* you'll live to a ripe old age, but what's in the future if

67

you don't marry and have children?"

"Did I say I would not?" He lifted one eyebrow with dark insolence. "I could be thinking of that very thing right now!"

She drew in her breath, being swept down a corridor with no end.

"Pity the woman!" The words came to her in a stunning flash.

"Just as you like!" he rejoined suavely.

As quickly as she was critical she was contrite, thinking of all he had done for her. "Oh, please, Steven," she said gently, "I didn't mean . . . you're getting me all wrong!"

"I'm getting you all *right*!" he said very crisply indeed, "though there are a few things about yourself you don't realise." He leant forward and switched on the ignition, not taking his eyes off her. They were pure *green*! All trace of blue had been washed out of them. She put a hand to her throat and tore her eyes away from him, knowing a swift thrust of warning. What idiocy was this? He had been right to advise her to put a curb on her emotions. He was cruel in a way, but he was honest, more absolute than she could ever be. Still, he was Steven! It became necessary to say something at once.

"I'll try not to bother you while I'm here," she said, her voice edged with sweet submission.

"Oh, come now, you improbable child!" his glance whipped across her and back to the road again. "Isn't that rather unnecessarily desperate? Besides, how do you propose to accomplish it? The fact is, you *do* bother me! You're too damned young and defenceless. That baby cap of curls and the trace of a scar showing through! The devil is, how to handle you . . ." he broke off in a low, amused voice. "Now for God's sake let's stop all this foolish chit-chat. Just remember to give in to me on every point and you'll be all right!"

"You're too single-minded!" she smiled, and there was some special magic in the way it showed up her teeth and her mouth and her eyes.

"Perhaps I am." He gave her a jewelled, sidelong glance. "Don't you think it unwise to capture so much of my attention?"

"Damn you, Steven!" She over-reacted to that mocking, ironic, speculative stare.

"That's more like it!" he jeered lightly. "Now look out the window like a good girl and you'll see some concrete evidence of my much-maligned single-mindedness. Go on," there was a soft taunt to his voice, "there's nothing at all to worry about!"

She looked away from that saturnine dark face that so plainly gave the lie to his words. The short twilight was setting in muting the glory of the sky. Soon it would turn to a soft purple. They were approaching a wide, pebbled drive that coiled in a circle around an avenue of scarlet-blossoming poinciana, the most beautiful tree of the tropics. She caught her breath and said quickly:

"Oh, please slow down!"

His low laugh touched her ears and the needle dropped back to cruising speed. If her life wasn't as untouched as a new fall of snow she would have said it was the most spectacular driveway she had ever seen in her life. The feathery, magnificent shade trees created a natural arch heavily festooned with flowers. Vast spreads of lawn slipped away on either side and right up to the house. Here was a more forceful symbol of Steven's reported wealth!

It loomed up ahead, gleaming white; a two-storied central section flanked on either side by single wings, with a long exquisite wrought iron lace balustrade running the full length of the veranda of the centre section. The drive arched before the house to lose itself in the winding lane of towering trees. Garden strips hugged the front of the house bright with massed colour, the heady perfumes of the tropics, and a beautiful jacaranda, its blossom spent, dominated the central bed, ringed round with luxuriant ferns and speckled lilies.

Steven drew abreast of the house and pulled up.

"This is it, little one. Welcome to Mokhana!" He got out and walked around to her side of the car to help her out. They walked up to the front of the house to where a golden subdued light came from an old colonial brass-bound carriage lamp of amber glass, that matched the floor-to-ceiling glass panels on either side of the massive cedar door. The door was open, and they stepped into an entrance hall that was a largish room in itself, hung with three impressionistic canvases that threw waves of colour about the walls with gemlike clarity. A lustrous cedar cabinet with fine carvings on the drawers and legs stood against one wall holding a copper urn full of beautiful, saffron-coloured lilies from the garden, with long trails of tiny bronze leaves that touched and were reflected in a carved trumeau that hung above it, decorated in gold leaf.

The gleaming parqueted floor was partially covered by a cream hand-woven wool rug decorated with elegant brown and black motifs and a runner of the same design carpeted the stairway that sprang up from the centre of the hallway and wound itself into the upper reaches of the next floor. Lights suddenly blossomed above them, a shadowless, deeply radiant illumination, coming from the striking modernistic light fitting of amber glass that matched the one that flared over the stairs.

Andrea looked up, unashamedly admiring, then heard for the first time a voice she was to come to know well.

"Steven darling, you're back! A good trip, I hope?"

Andrea tensed and looked towards the top of the stairs. It was odd, but the voice gave her a flick of pain like the old throb in her head wound.

A woman stood at the head of the stairs, the light glancing off her coal-black head, silvered, almost theatrically but quite naturally, in narrow silver wings over the temples She bore no particular resemblance to Steven beyond the fact that she was tall and dark and she had his stunning self-assurance.

Steven looked up, the amber glow sheening his dark face.

"Hello, my dear. We're a little earlier than I anticipated, but all to the good. A tail wind! This is Andrea, of course. My Aunt Helena, Andrea! "

Helena Daintree came on down the stairs, a tall regal sort of woman dressed in a very plain but beautifully cut hostess gown in heavy topaz silk. She gave Andrea her hand, subjecting her to a piercing, dark-eyed scrutiny, then she gave a faint smile.

"But really, darling, you were quite right! She's such a child, and so fragile! Welcome to Mokhana, my dear."

Andrea took all this with absolute gravity, knowing full well that she would never in a lifetime come close to this coolly reserved woman. "How do you do, Miss Daintree," she answered politely with a quick exchange of courtesies. "It was very kind of you to have me! "

"Steven's idea, child," Helena Daintree pointed out with a quick, secretive little glance at her nephew, "but naturally, I'm only too pleased to do what I can. You look very tired, but that's only to be expected." She turned her sleek head, the dark waves pulsing like coals. "Steven, there are one or two things that need your immediate attention. I wouldn't bother you, but I don't think they can wait. I've left a list under the paperweight on your desk. I'll take Andrea out to her room and settle her in." She turned to look into Andrea's pale face, the grey eyes tender and translucent but undeniably shadowed.

Steven broke in on his aunt as though he had only then begun to concentrate. "Out?" he queried rather tautly. "Where have you put her, then?"

"Why, the guest suite, dear!" Helena Daintree said, her own voice faintly incredulous. "She'll be completely private, with everything she could need to hand!"

Steven clamped down on a small sound of annoyance. "I told Netta expressly to prepare the Almond Room."

With an almost physical act of will Helena Daintree took the correction. "Yes, I know, dear, but . . ."

"Much the better idea!" Steven assured her. "See to it, would you, Helena? The guest wing is far too isolated. I don't want Andrea there. She's not nearly well enough to be on her own. She could call out in the night or anything and not a damn soul to hear her!"

"Well, of course, my dear." Helena Daintree gave a faint laugh that could have been a gasp under different circumstances. "I just didn't realise how very frail she is."

"No harm done," Steven answered evenly. "The room is kept aired in any case. You might take Andrea up and I'll bring up her things in a moment. I suppose I'd better leave a message with Freedman. Andrea might need a check-up from time to time."

Andrea found that her fingers were curled tightly into her palms. Her mind was blurring with tiredness, a wealth of new impressions, and her scant colour had faded. Steven dropped a hard hand on to her shoulder and she raised her face with a look of withdrawal, yet she yearned and yearned for the hard wall of his strength.

"You'd better go up to your room, child," he said with faint violence. "You look desperately tired all of a sudden. We'll dispense with dinner for tonight. A tray in your room, then an early night, perhaps a sedative. It was an over-long trip, I know, but I wanted to get you here as soon as possible!"

The vibrating warmth of him was communicated to her through his fingertips unconsciously caressing her collarbone. She fought the wildest impulse to let herself go completely limp against him. To be swept up into those hard, strong arms, to look up to see Steven's face, the aquamarine glitter of his strange, light eyes.

"Well, come along, then, dear!" Helena Daintree prompted in her dry, precise voice, her dark eyes very keen and watchful. "You've had quite an experience one way or the other. It's just impossible to cope with too many things at once!"

Steven smiled briefly down on her, then he was gone, striding through the hallway towards his study, and Andrea was left feeling marooned on a high plateau with his aunt.

"I hope you'll be happy here, Andrea," she said, following the direction of Andrea's gaze, her own stare shrewd and assessing. "I believe you had rather a time of it with the Goddens. They were anxious to have you?"

"Yes, they were." Andrea found herself looking away from that dark, questing glance, but found the nerve to add: "But Steven wouldn't hear of it!"

"Men always think they know best!" was Helena's answer, accompanied by a tight-lipped smile that plainly added she, herself, knew much better. With sudden clarity Andrea realised that her proposed convalescence on Mokhana was decidedly not Helena Daintree's decision, though she would have had the wisdom not to veto the

73

suggestion. She came back to earth to hear the older woman saying:

"However, you can always put things right when you're able. After all, I quite see Irina Godden's point of view, even if she is a neurotic, over-indulged woman. You *were* her son's fiancée!"

Rather desperately now and a shade curtly, Andrea murmured:

"If you don't mind, Miss Daintree, many things don't exist for me any more, and I find trying to discuss them particularly distressing when I'm tired."

For a moment Helena Daintree looked decidedly taken back by this unexpected show of spirit. Something flickered in her night-dark eyes, then she was all contrition, a state of being that sat oddly on her. "But of course, my dear. How thoughtless of me! Steven did *warn me!*"

She let that peculiar statement trail up in the air, allowing Andrea to draw any conclusion she liked, then turned and led the way up the stairs along a cool, wide corridor of pale walls and lighted cornices glowing down on what was almost an art gallery. Someone in the house was quite obviously a collector. Was it Steven or his aunt? Probably both, Andrea concluded.

Much as she wanted to stand and stare, and to her faint bewilderment she was familiar with one particular style, she was even more anxious to get to her room.

Just let me get there! she thought rather feverishly. It would be a relief to be on her own. There was no need to pretend. She found Helena Daintree overpowering. Perhaps tomorrow she could be more able to cope with this tall, rather coldly imperious woman. In the meantime there was nothing to be afraid of, nothing to hurt her. Not with Steven!

Helena Daintree paused before a pale green door,

moulded in a darker shade, then opened it with a swift burst of decision.

"Here we are!" she said briskly. "I hope you like it. To some tastes, *not* mine, it's the most beautiful room in the house. I can't pretend to agree. It was Vivienne's — Steven's mother's. Her style exactly. Not mine, as I've said, though I've often wanted to alter it, to bring it more into keeping with my own style which I feel is appropriately elegant but functional. This room quite clearly is *not!*"

Andrea could only agree. She touched a reverent toe to the deeply piled white carpet.

"I've had it treated, of course," Helena Daintree said dryly, glancing downwards. "Such a hopeless colour, nevertheless!" She stood back and allowed Andrea to precede her into the room.

At first, Andrea couldn't conceive of anything more lovely, not realising at first that there was no place for a man in a room such as this. It was, quite startlingly, a feminine shrine, a haven and a refuge. There was no place at all for a husband or a small son. She was only conscious of almond green drapes at the windows, the sheer central fall of white lace, the matching quilted almond green silk of the bedspread; of exquisite period furniture of blossoming colours in a watercolour, the damasked wall paper, two deep armchairs upholstered in varietoned silks of blue and green, a low antique table set with precious knick-knacks, a slim bookcase, and against the window wall, a delicate writing desk with a head of a small boy cast in bronze and small collection of family portraits.

"It's quite beautiful," she said almost dreamily. And it was ! Finished right down to the last detail.

"I thought you might say that!" Helena Daintree

maintained, and her dry voice seemed to carry a wasp's sting. "Certainly it's more your style than mine. The intensely feminine conception, I suppose. Not everyone's cup of tea!" She let her glance pass over the room with total disinterest, then she walked towards the centre of the room with the wary tread of a cat.

"There's a walk-in wardrobe beyond this mirrored door." She moved to open it out, indicating the light switch within. "You'll have plenty of room for your things, as you can see. The bathroom is at the end of the hall on the same side as this. You'll have to share with me. Steven has his own suite, of course. If you're anything like me you'll like to spread out. I do have such a collection of jars and lotions and whatnot. You could in that case use the guest suite, I suppose, if you'd like to put out your own things."

Andrea nodded her head, taking the hint easily. Helena Daintree wasn't the kind of woman to share anything with anyone! Even in the midst of her tiredness she spared a thought for the defecting Vivienne who had sought another life. Perhaps she had been driven to it? Who would know, and she was too exhausted to speculate. It was almost impossible to imagine the kind of woman who could live for any length of time in harmony with Helena Daintree, unless she was a complete doormat. Aware that she was tensed and that tenseness led to headaches, she tried to relax again.

"If you're quite all right now, my dear," the older woman said affably, "I'll go to Steven. He may need me!" Behind that gracious smile some faint struggle was taking place. "Tomorrow, when you're feeling rested, we'll go on a tour of the house," she promised. "It's rather large, as you can see, but we do have a lot of visitors to put up from time to time. Quite without notice, usually.

They just fly in, on business, mostly, and the occasional overseas visitor wished on us by the powers that be!"

As if it were of no consequence she added casually, "Until tomorrow, then, my dear. Sleep well! I'll send one of the girls up with your tray. We have quite a big staff and all of them well organised. Two of our girls wait at table, two others help Sam Tong, our cook, in the kitchen. There's a great deal of baking required to keep the stockmen supplied with scones and cakes and whatnots for smokos. Then there's the laundry, the housework and the vegetable garden to look after. They're very well trained, even if I do say so myself! "

Andrea didn't need that light emphasis. She could well see Helena Daintree was admirably suited to training people. She managed a faint answering smile that held, had she known it, a totally adult perception; an awareness of the older woman's personality and its demands.

"I'll be quite happy in this beautiful room. Thank you once again, Miss Daintree!"

"Don't mention it, my dear. Just get better soon!"

She was gone with a swirl of her heavy silken skirts and Andrea sank down on the bed for a moment, smiling with a certain wry amusement. What Helena Daintree should have said was: the sooner the better! but perhaps the gracious hostess couldn't really allow such a sledgehammer approach. In any case, if one was tired and sensitive it didn't seem to matter over-much. The message was the same. It was difficult to become enthusiastic about such a reception. Irina Godden, at least, really wanted her! But always and for ever there was Steven. He had made the decision and she had obeyed.

There was a tap at the door and the momentum of her thoughts dropped away. She called "Come in!" and the door opened to reveal a pert, dusky-skinned young woman in a neat blue button-through dress with immaculate collar and cuffs.

"Evenin', miss! I'm Netta!" She smiled, displaying perfect, even, white teeth. "Would you like me to unpack for you? You're tired, I expect."

"Are my cases there, Netta?" Andrea asked, half rising from the bed.

"Yes, miss, just outside the door. Mr. Tong brought them up. Mr. Steven said!"

"That's very kind of you, Netta," Andrea smiled, conveying a quality of warmth and appreciation that made the coloured girl for ever her friend.

"No trouble at all, miss," Netta said sweetly. "I'm mighty quick. *And* neat! Don't I have to be!" A kind of merry, racial humour was evident in every line of her pretty young face, the glossy black eyes startlingly white-ringed. She spun on her heel, injecting a great deal of breathtaking energy into bringing in the cases one by one and propping them up beside the bed.

"Now you just take a seat over there and I'll turn back the bed. Seems a shame to mess it up, don't it? Pretty enough for a dream or the pictures or something!" Her small face screwed up. "It belonged to Miss Vivienne, so old Minna says, and she knows everything! But that was a pretty desperate situation, as I understand."

Andrea struggled up from the bed and into an armchair, her interest fairly caught.

"What was, Netta?"

Netta turned, not even having to consider. "Why, Miss Vivienne," she said urgently, her soft voice rising. "She jus' up and left 'em, but that was a long time ago." She looked at Andrea in a rare burst of speculation. "You a friend of Mr. Steve's?"

"I hope so!" Andrea smiled.

Netta folded her arms snugly across her chest. "I expect you are, 'cause he wanted you to have the Almond Room and that's *this*!" She looked towards Andrea earnestly. "No one, but no one, is allowed in here. Even herself, the missus, that is!"

"Well, I like it!" Andrea said suddenly.

Netta laughed and with deft movements had the quilted silk spread neatly folded along the end of the bed. She flipped back the pale green satin-bound blankets to reveal flower-sprigged percale sheets and matching pillow cases, doing a series of turns before confronting Andrea with a serene grin, her liquid eyes gleaming.

"See? Made it up jus' like Mr. Steve said!" She paused for effect. "He's the boss around here. What do you think?"

Andrea shook her head. "I guess so!" she said weakly, then she began to laugh in soft, muffled gurgles which drew forth Netta's approving grin. Netta was now energetically striding back and forth from the opened suitcases to the bureau and the adjoining walk-in wardrobe, humming a snatch of an outdated tune. She bent to pick up a nightgown, a misty froth of sea-jade, and it was impossible not to smile at the expression on her face. She ran an awed finger across a filmy fold, then placed it at the head of the bed on the pillow, arranging a matching lace-bordered peignoir meticulously beside it. The choice taken out of her hands, Andrea sat back deciding she must wear it.

Netta was silent a moment, mulling something over, then she called over her shoulder, respect deepening her voice.

"You sure have a lot of money, miss," she asserted, devoutly pleased with herself and her deductions. "Even Miss Helena don't have no better than this. Why, something like this could make a girl flip!"

Andrea burst out laughing at the absurdity of the situation. For a long time she stared at the nightgown with the puzzling but certain conviction that she had never indulged in such an expensive item in her life. Indeed half of the clothes Netta carried to and fro were arousing much the same sensations in her as in Netta. The little coloured girl worked on, oblivious to Andrea's thoughtful stares, a look of great satisfaction on her face, making little unconsciously humorous comments on this and that, running her fingers carefully and lovingly over the materials that made a sensuous appeal to her. Finally she disappeared into the wardrobe to pack away the empty suitcases.

"Somethin' delicious coming up in about ten minutes!" she promised, reappearing. "You'll be crazy about Mr. Tong's cooking. It's really out of sight! In fact, I expect you'll get fat. You could do with a little meat on them bones. You look like the dawn wind blew you in puffing right at your heels!" She turned a perfectly mischievous face over her shoulder and walked to the door.

"Evenin', Miss Andrea. Anything I can do for you, you just sing out!"

Andrea lay back in the armchair, her grey eyes luminous with laughter. Netta had had an exhilarating effect on her. From somewhere in the house came the tranquil, melodious chime of a clock. She lay back, her eyes closing.

As Netta had promised, the light meal when it arrived was not only delicious but beautifully presented, but Andrea found herself picking at the creamed chicken and mushrooms, the tiny golden brown potato balls, the small portion of tossed salad, for appearances only. Her appetite seemed to have deserted her and it would take all of the fabled Mr. Tong's resources to coax it back again. She dipped her spoon into the chilled fruit cocktail, finding the pineapple unexpectedly flavoured with brandy. To her surprise she finished it, leaving only the maraschino cherry.

Afterwards the house seemed very quiet and for that one night she decided to run her bath in Helena's private sanctum with its adjoining dressing room; all mirrors, natural timber fittings and ceramic wall tiles in opaline tints. She avoided stepping on the pale, lovely rugs that were scattered on the floor, letting her eyes wander over a vast collection of jars; the cleansing creams, the day creams, the night cream, the eye creams, the vitamin-enriched creams, the mounds of expensive soap in hanging baskets, the squat bottles, the tall bottles, the black bottles and the crystal bottles containing bath salts and various oils. It just could have been a display counter at one of the better stores, Andrea reflected, a little surprised that Helena Daintree was included among the ranks of women for whom preservation of their good looks had developed into a career.

She didn't linger over her bath as she would have liked to but reached for the huge, velvety towel, one of two Netta had placed in her room. She looked up absently and caught sight of herself in the wall-to-wall mirror opposite; the ashen blonde hair feathering damply around her head, one white arm raised to hold the enveloping towel. She looked all eyes, much too thin, the slim girl's body still haunted by fragility. She shrugged a delicate shoulder and withdrew her critical, examining eyes from her reflection. Miracles didn't happen overnight. She was lucky to have escaped with her life.

Once back in her room she found it difficult to settle down. Her heart and her brain were too keyed up. She felt shatteringly alone. She wandered over to the writing desk and picked up the small, over-shaped portraits one by one.

A faint secret essence clung to this room, to the old photographs, as if the young Vivienne must once have attached a lot of importance to them. Two of the photographs were old-fashioned, stiffly posed studies of a man and a woman in Court dress, looking suitably elegant; the third was undeniably the small boy, Steven, his happy, carefree face showing the promise of the man to come. It was a first-rate piece of photography and she held it for a long time. The last could only have been Garth Daintree, a little of Steven, a great deal more of his sister in those lean, dark features. He looked a hard man, Andrea thought, even among men of legendary hardness, but he *was* handsome. She put the photograph back on the desk, placing it with the same fastidious care Steven's mother might have shown.

"Poor Vivienne!" she said to herself, knowing it was her heart, not her head, that prompted her. She glanced down at the last item, the small bronze head, noticing for the first time the cut of the profile. Her heart rocked and she picked it up, warming the cold bronze against her hand. How indescribably precious! The face of innocence, of childhood – of Steven. There was a knock on the door and her heart seemed to give a great bound so that it fluttered right up into her throat.

"Andrea!"

She heard his voice, quiet but implacable. For the life of her she was unable to answer, held in the grip of some nerve-racking emotion. Then, just as some measure of release came to her, he thrust open the door, looking across the intervening space, his eyes glittering under the lids.

"Good God, child, you might have answered!" His

voice was a mixture of anxiety, a faint bewilderment and some exasperation. He held a glass of water and a phial of tablets in his hand.

Ordinarily she would have answered him, but at that moment she seemed stunned and silent, holding the small bronze head between her breasts, her shoulders pale and tender slightly bent.

"What's the matter?" He came to her and held her, gripping her shoulders with a fierce kind of necessity, a hard mixture of tenderness and violence. She stared up at him helplessly, with some weak feeling, a deep inner trembling, half ache, half longing, creeping, stealthily, robber-like through her veins.

"Andrea, answer me!" He shook her slightly and only some reserve of will power kept her poised away from him when all she wanted to do was lay her head against his chest and hear the soft thud of his heart. His face seemed all angled planes and shadows, his eyes brilliantly alive, sending her swirling down a racing stream of jagged currents and submerged rocks. She could never, never drift quietly with Steven. Everything about him, his physical aura, his personality, was making that impossible.

Her head was tilted back, the light glinting on her hair, probing the sea-green robe, its fragility covering yet revealing the ivory curve of a shoulder, the narrow taut waist, the tilt of a breast. He gave a muffled exclamation and looked down at her hands, gripping tightly on the bronze head against all other temptations.

"Well, well! Don't tell me this little thing has all that much significance?" There was a hard, mocking, quality to his voice that hurt her, cutting close to her heart.

"It's you, isn't it?" she said with soft poignancy. No

question but a statement, her face turned towards him.

"I was never quite certain!"

She felt the tension in him, but his tone, the faint ironic smile, the set of his dark head, were barbs to taunt her.

"Oh yes, it's you!" she repeated firmly. "There's a whole world of love in this little head."

"I prefer to call it professional expertise," he said curtly, more to himself than to her. "A facility only!"

"That's cruel, Steven!" She traced a gentle finger over the tender young profile.

"Cruel as the truth often is," he said flatly and without warmth.

"You'll never get me to agree!" She lifted her head, her eyes suddenly sparkling like crystal chips.

His smile hardened. "So ethereal a creature to show a little spirit!" That dark insolence was back on him. She tried to speak, but suddenly, startlingly, could not.

He took the bronze from her hands, gripped with such nervous intensity and placed it behind them on the desk. There were shadows in the hollows of her cheeks, beneath her large, tilting eyes, her hair curling like silvery wood shavings about her small head.

"You should be in bed," he said harshly. "The whole day's been too much for you. Get in, like a good girl, and I'll give you your tablet."

His dark head was bent over her. She seemed bound, helpless, captive, and he suddenly swung her up into his arms, cradling her head. The sweet heady scents of the garden drifted through the open windows and they were alone, isolated, sheafed in the muted quiet. She relaxed against him, filled with an exhausted kind of sweetness, making no protest as the peignoir whispered off her shoulders. Then she was lying back in the bed and he was placing the filmy folds over the end of the bed.

"It's not mine, is it?" she asked with a soft, butterfly sigh.

"Well, it's not *mine*!" He wheeled, a dry note in his voice.

She lifted a pale hand across her eyes. "I knew I couldn't have bought one half of those things!"

He came to stand beside the bed, with a look of brooding concentration. "You had precious little left of your own. Whatever you travelled with was lost in the wreckage. What else would you have had me do?"

He sounded faintly harassed and she looked up at his jewel-coloured eyes.

"I'm terribly in your debt, aren't I, Steven? Hopelessly so!"

"You little fool!" His voice flicked at her like a whip. The light was behind his dark head and powerful shoulders giving him a look of turbulent vitality, almost menace.

"It would be so easy to hate you!" she breathed, her eyes narrowing defensively at the sight of him.

"How are you going to convince me of that?"

"I can't answer that!" Her suddenly impassioned voice betrayed her agitation.

"Why? Are you afraid?"

It was intolerable to have him so near and so far away from her.

"No, no! of course not! I . . . I . . . just don't know."

"Then I'll help you find out!" he said grimly. "It's quite simple really."

Her heart was a bright trapped bird beating futilely against its cage. She couldn't turn her face away even if he would have permitted her to do so. She could only stare up at him, memorising that dark face, the combination of line and feature and colour, the exact blue-green of his eyes. She was drugged, almost drowning in a strange dreamlike fantasy with the queer feeling of having looked into that face so many, many times before. There was no one else like Steven. There never would be again. She was entirely quiescent, her face betraying her emotions, defeated by her own intensely feminine nature.

He made some brief, muffled exclamation, then lowered his head abruptly, darkly, vividly handsome, and she closed her eyes against him, giving herself up to the tumultuous shock of his mouth. Her own mouth was parting under that wild, fierce pressure, the bewildering, questing intensity. She was sinking, sinking into a soft, purple darkness where her mind and her heart seemed countless aeons apart.

Time and place lost all meaning, there was no logic to anything, only a shattering, never-to-be-borne excitement the sounds of the night ... and Steven. Her pale hands were locked behind his head, but she didn't know it until he jerked his head back with stunning force, leaving her bereft, holding down her wrists implacably.

"I didn't bring you out of one jungle to get into *this*!" he said brutally. "It's senseless, and it won't happen again!"

The colour raced under her pale translucent skin. "No, it won't, because I won't be here long enough!" She tried to struggle up with a flash of the girl she had been before pain and danger had catapulted into her life, but he held her back against his arm, a lick of flame in his eyes, giving her fair warning not to challenge him.

"There's no way at all you'll leave Mokhana before *I* say so," he said tautly, "even if my own damned idea has boomeranged on me."

The strangeness of his voice made her wary. Her eyes

were as huge and velvety as a faun, a soft almond blossom bloom on her cheekbones.

"Let me go, Steven," she said much too reasonably. "Let's say good night, please!"

"Oh, let's say good night by all means," he mimicked her. "Do you think it a joke, the way you react to a man?"

"Why are you so kind, then so . . . brutal to me?" she demanded, and drew a single, indrawn breath.

His dark brows shot up. "Because I'm *that* kind of a man. Demoralizing, I know, but I did warn you!" He sounded grim, his eyes scanning the narrow outline of her body.

"Oh, please, Steven!" she said on a soft protest. "I must be alone."

"I'll leave you alone, don't worry, but don't waste your time trying to run away from me."

"On my honour!" she said, her soft mouth still pulsing from the pressure of his. "Nothing's real, is it?" she asked, her voice overwrought like a child's. "I don't know what to do any more!" Her carefully hidden excitement was showing in the density of colour in her eyes, her cheeks, her mouth, the nightgown falling off her shoulder more innocent than seductive because of the tender hollows.

Unaccountably his face lost its hard, watchful look, and his mouth twisted faintly.

"Such melodrama! You'll be good, that's all!"

He looked so careless and mocking that her heart turned in her breast. She stared back at him, excitement rising like waves along the whole length of her from her feet to the top of her head. A love and a hate and a fury! For yes, she *loved* him with a force that was shocking to her. A whole world of insanity when Steven had no need of such cloying sentimentality. He had no need of the enduring love of a woman. Not with that arrogant cut of the mouth and the nostrils, the jewelled flash of his eyes, the imperious set of his head.

The air was electric between them and they were speaking in undertones.

"Damn you, Steven!" she gasped, her voice pitched above the wild beating of her heart. "My only hope is that some woman puts you through hell!" Her eyes were shimmering in her lovely flushed face and his eyes narrowed dangerously:

"Why don't you find the courage to try yourself?" he goaded her. "After all, you've made a good start!"

She drew back from the glitter of his eyes, so coldly brilliant that it hurt her to look at him. He suddenly caught her chin, kissing her parted, throbbing mouth, a brief contact so different in quality, a tender punishment, not a tyranny, that her eyes filled with tears, diamond bright.

"Life's terrible, isn't it, little one, now that you're withdrawing from your dream world?"

She threw herself over on her face, shutting out his physical presence, the frightening delight that it gave her, but his hand touched the nape of her neck, like a brand on her skin.

"That won't help. Come on, turn around and be brave. I only want you to take your tablet," he said mockingly.

He was no longer the same and she was free to turn back to him. "You're making things hard for me," she said plaintively.

"I know!" The laugh sounded in his voice and he was at the back of her, helping her, though she could have managed herself. She took the glass and her hand trembled.

"I don't want to be brave. I don't want to be anything!" she said like an overwrought child.

"You *do*!" He handed her the tablet and watched her swallow it, making a wry face. "You want to be a good, sweet little girl, I just know it!" His eyes slid over her face and her throat and it was suddenly unbearable not to turn back into his arms.

"For *you*, Steven," she said with faint bitterness, "I could promise anything!"

His voice was carefully controlled, a shade caustic, but his eyes fairly blazed.

"When you're fit enough I'll let you say that again. Anything is likely to come of it!"

The blood rushed to her head, but he was gone with his quick, lithe tread, walking to the door shutting it on her with a half savage:

"Good night, little one, sleep well and give all that emotionalism a rest!"

She was alone at last, left with the memory of those moments of excitement and exultation when his mouth had moved on her own.

CHAPTER V

THE weeks drifted by, relaxed and lazy in the heat and exotica of the tropics. Though Steven allowed her to do very little, he saw to it that she was never bored. She could read. She could laze in the sun for a short period, then back to the cushioned lounger with its striped awning in the shade of the giant tamarinds. She could, if Netta accompanied her, swim in the far end of the Pink Lily Lagoon, but never on her own, for Steven appeared to regard her as a semi-precious incompetent, or as she put it to him herself . . . an idiot relation. With a brief flash of white teeth in a dark, devastating face he denied it. She was to be watched, that was all, until she was completely well. Netta was a delightful and endearing companion and she was by far the most intelligent and reliable of all the girls.

Steven's attitude, Andrea found, hovered drastically between a conscientious big brother and wildly unsettling glimpses of the man, Steven. Those moments, increasingly rare, made every nerve in her body scream for release, arousing a torrent of crazy notions that just as suddenly he went out of his way to crush. It was a deliberate manoeuvre, for he told her she was as transparent to him as the delicate tracery of blue veins under her skin.

He was kind. He was considerate. He was maddening. He was Steven, inflicting pleasure and pain of a kind. Sometimes when he was able, he took her out for short trips about the property or called down on her when she went swimming with Netta, his eyes approving the fine gleam of pale gold that overlaid her satiny skin.

Each morning she breakfasted in bed whether she liked

it or not, filled in her day pleasantly, made a creditable attempt to dispose of an invariably excellent dinner, for Steven watched her like a hawk, then she retired early. That was the pattern of every day, and a new one began like the other. If she sometimes fell prone to anguishes or reticences Steven was able to bring her out of it with a word or a lift of his dark brows, for he seemed to be continually on the lookout for some such disturbances. The great thing was, he said, she was regaining her strength and natural vitality, and she *had* put on a few much-needed pounds of body weight.

Her relationship with Helena Daintree continued as it had begun, with a carefully maintained courtesy on both sides. There could be no question of a little warmth being injected into the situation, for the older woman made it plain, without words, that no such thing was required. Andrea was Steven's guest, and her love and devotion to her nephew was quite obviously deeply embedded. On this account Andrea had the certain feeling that she was tolerated and treated to the best Mokhana could offer, which was, in a nutshell, a very great deal. And so life went on with every physical comfort and the stimulation of an environment that was strange to her, doubly so, for she had no clear recollection of another.

Yet there were compensations galore! The beauty of Mokhana, after the Wet, was breathtaking! Partly arising from the brilliance of the sun and the sky, the lush greens of the grasslands, the sleek, prime cattle with their glistening hides, the tropical splendour of the blossoming trees and flowers and partly from the sharp contours of the smoky blue to indigo ranges, the strange aura of the rain forest that loomed over their boundaries. The bird life, too, was fantastic and drew Andrea's attention as it did everyone from the city, for Mokhana was paradise! Great flocks of budgerigar took to the skies, darkening the sun, wheeling and diving in formation over the still waters of the lakes and lagoons and the silent billabongs, a blinding sheen of emerald glinting off breasts and wings. There were rose pink galahs in almost equal numbers, black cockatoos with red, iridescent tail feathers, the white cockatoos with their singular sulphur crests, the legions of tiny jewelled finches, and the opal-tinted parrots and lorikeets, the waterfowl without number, the eagles and hawks that circled the cloudless intense blue of the skies.

Before long Andrea found she had developed an uncanny observation that surprised and delighted Netta, who by heritage and long experience had the closest communion with nature, and could read every sign like the lines on her hand. From the birds Andrea progressed to the tropical flora, intrigued by the beauty and profusion of the floating lotus blooms, waxy bursts of ivory, violet blue and palest pink and the native orchids with their eerie, exotic fascination. Steven, though anything but insensitive to the beauty of his great selection, because he was born to it and took such things for granted, spent most of his day on practicalities and the hundred and one problems besetting a huge station. So the weeks went by with nothing to disturb the easy harmony he seemed bent on maintaining. If Andrea yearned for a more demanding relationship, life on Mokhana was still full of flavour.

About a month later when she was out with Netta on one of the short walkabouts Steven permitted, Dr. Freedman arrived for a short visit. Seeing the Cessna fly in and more or less expecting some such visit, Andrea left Netta collecting wild honey and made her way back to the house, hurrying in the heat, something Steven had always stressed she was not to. She wasn't surprised in the least when the jeep ground to a halt beside her and he swung out his lower lip tightly between his teeth.

There was a moment of dead silence while his glittery glance flashed over her with hard watchfulness, noting the swift reflex action of tilting her head and squaring her shoulders.

"Aha, aha!" she said flippantly, the pupils of her eyes dilating, "I suppose I'm in for a lecture?"

"Aha, aha, indeed!" he caught the point of her shoulder, spinning it into the jeep like a doll. "A typical schoolgirl reaction. Where in sweet hell is your hat?"

Stoically she kept her head tilted up to him. "There's no need to get agitated. I never freckle!"

"*Freckle!*" he broke in, malicious and mocking. "Such a side effect is purely coincidental. I'm talking about sun-stroke!"

"Oh, really, Steven," she managed, low-voiced. "Sometimes you act like a great watchdog ready to pounce!"

"What do you expect?" he clipped out the syllables. "I brought you out here to look after you and that's still my intention, seeing you can't look after yourself. Surely Netta had the sense to make you take a hat?"

"She *did!*" she said despairingly. "It's full of boronia, as a matter of fact. I was going to dry out the petals. I just happened to look up and see the Cessna come in, so I hurried."

He made a jeering sound, his brilliant gaze downright hostile. "The Cessna, why not? I'll accept that. After all, it's not every day your boy-friend comes calling."

"What boy-friend?" she demanded, her eyes suddenly sparkling in contrast to their usual soft shimmer.

He studied her in silence for a moment – the silver-gilt head, the palest gold skin tints, the apricot flush of sun spots high up on her cheekbones. "I do believe he'll find a change in you. From a snow maiden to a silver blonde, kissed by the sun. He'll probably want to do the same himself," he added cynically, "but you'd better warn him off in advance. There's nothing doing in that direction!"

She looked away from the carved mockery of his lean, dark features. "I thought one was supposed to fall in with what the doctor ordered!"

"Not in this case, little one," he said with soft menace. "I'd keep those lake-coloured eyes to yourself. The good doctor has more than half drowned in them already."

"How ridiculous!" she sank her teeth in her bottom lip, colouring it cherry.

"Yes, isn't it?" he stressed briefly. "I'm glad you agree, it will save a certain unpleasantness all round."

She flickered a glance at his profile and found it inaccessible. "You're more than usually arrogant this morning," she said, greatly daring.

"I'm more than usually a lot of things, but I wouldn't expect you to see it!" A hard mocking light flared in his eyes.

She clenched a small fist in her lap. "I can't for the life of me see why you want to put up with me!" Tension showed itself in the fine-boned oval of her face, and she was conscious of an element of excitement and danger between them.

He muffled an oath and grasped her pale nape, his fingers biting into her flesh. "Listen, you silly child, I just don't want you exploited – your beauty exploited, though you might find it hard to believe."

He was hurting her, unconscious of his strength, and she put up a hand to his arm, feeling a sick shiver of excitement.

94

"What if the doctor is *serious*? What then?" she taunted him, knowing she was doing violence to herself just trying to rouse a response in him.

His eyes narrowed to slits and the line of his jaw hardened. "Well then, that's just too damned bad! Now sit back and stop trying to earn yourself some reprisals. I'll take you down to the strip as part of the welcoming party. I wouldn't like the good doctor to think I was keeping you all to myself!"

"Well, that's hardly the case, is it?" she said with brittle irony.

He looked dangerous, darkly relentless, his blue-green gaze whipping over her face, lingering on the pulse that beat so frantically at the base of her throat. "If you'd been older, a little wiser, who knows?" he said in an oddly taut tone. "As it is, you're just an over-emotional child!"

"There's really no need to keep cutting me down to size," she said tightly. "I just hope something horrible will happen to you!"

"Do you?" A kind of hard recklessness lay on him like a patina of light. He reached for her suddenly and pulled her across his knees, watching the flame of fear gather in her eyes. "Fate's played one too many tricks on me already!"

Her satiny skin was suffused with colour and she flung up one hand to hit out at him, hating him, *hating him*, her very skin tingling to his touch, unbearably hurt by his cynicism.

"It couldn't last, could it?" he ground out harshly, and she felt herself go white with the shock of it, her slight body against his feeling the dark, frightening energy that fed his anger. She made a small sound that died in her throat as his hand sank into her curls, dragging her head back. He kissed her into a shaken and breathless submission where there was no place left to retreat to, his hand curled in possession over the curve of her breast.

A soft shiver ran through her like an arrowhead of flame, and she moved against him so that he relented his cruel hold, shaping the back of her neck, his mouth deepening its pressure, leaving a track of fire across her face and throat. Her shining head was thrown back against the hard curve of his shoulder, its sensitive modelling heightened by emotion, her eyes tightly closed, the heavy lashes wet.

He lifted his dark head, his glance striking her face. There was, instantly, anger and arrogance and something without name in the flare of his nostrils, the startling onrush of colour into his eyes.

"Don't cry!" The order was curt, compulsive, his voice offering no apology. "You brought this all on yourself. Just how much of this day-to-day teasing did you think I could take?"

Her voice was muffled up with a kind of pain. "But I never ... I haven't!" She turned her head helplessly in amazement and distress, then opened her eyes to find his, pitilessly mocking, pinning her to a blue-green infinity.

"The number one rule," he said with hard cynicism. "Never expect honesty from a woman. They have no ethics in that small matter and never, *never* assume one of them entirely innocent. You know damned well you've been asking for that!"

"You're so *right!*" she said bitterly, driven by his hard, infuriating expression, realising with sudden shame that some strange force kept her within the circle of his arm. Belatedly she tried to break free, but his fingers bit into her soft shoulder, tightening his hold, using his strength deliberately, for mastery. Her eyes, abnormally large and brilliant, shimmering like ice crystals, began to well swiftly with tears; an acute femininity that made his white teeth snap together, his voice rough edged with curbed violence.

"Don't *do* that!"

Her strange little laugh was like a bell in her throat. "No, you can't stand it, can you? I wonder why? The hard, the superior, the relentless, the so self-sufficient Steven Daintree! I'm *glad* you can't stand it!" Into her voice shot a tremor of panic.

His hand closed under her chin and an alien light flared in his eyes, the second shock scarcely less brutal than the first.

"You've nothing *yet* to cry about!" he said, his glance slanting unpleasantly over her, "but there's no guarantee that will last!"

A white-hot tension shot through her, shocking her back to reality. A thin stratum of her mind registered there was a devil aroused in him, that she had never glimpsed before his eyes flashing warning signals, an element of danger she didn't choose to analyse. The taste of salt was in her mouth, her face burning hot.

"Oh, please, Steven!" Her eyes were fixed on his face with a direct plea for understanding, but he didn't withdraw his hand, his face dark and taut with the unyielding look of polished steel. Blindly she nudged his hand aside to turn her hot face into his throat, aching for comfort, a fever burning in her. "Don't be like this, please! I can't bear it. I'd never want anything horrible to happen to you, you know that. You just throw me off balance. I can't explain!"

Something of what she was feeling must have got through to him, for his hand dropped to her creamy, vulnerable nape, this time exquisitely gentle, and the burden of alarm was lifted.

"The easy way you get out of it. *Please, Steven, I can't bear it!* Child into woman. Woman into child, and so convenient!" His hand fell to caressing the line of her neck, his heart storming into her own, a wild kind of music that was almost a torment.

"I can't go with you *now!*" she said shakily.

"You will!" His hand stilled on her skin.

"I can't! Oh, please, Steven!" She lifted her face to him, her expression transparent, and his eyes struck down rather grimly on the curve of her mouth with its tell-tale trembling.

"No, perhaps not!" he said, the dark, brooding look back on his face. "I'll take you back to the house. Give you a little time to assume another personality – a simple enough feat for a woman!"

He put her away from him abruptly with unmistakable renunciation, his glance now cool, with an analytical detachment almost that of a near-stranger. "I'm damned if I know what you are. A doe-eyed innocent, Godden's fiancée . . . what? In short, little one, you present a problem!"

"I shall run away!" she said tragically, the midday sun blazing down on her head.

Incredibly a smile transfigured his face, mocking points of light dancing in his eyes. His glance slid softly over her from head to toe. "You wouldn't get very far! I've inexhaustible patience when something interests me, and you, Andrea, are a very intriguing study. I can't bear to let you out of my sight!"

Beyond his imperious dark head was a boundless blue space she could fix her attention on. A respite, however, brief.

"One of these days, Steven," she said softly, "you're going to get your just deserts!"

98

He shrugged one powerful shoulder, his brilliant eyes glittering over her. "If it makes you feel any better, just keep on hoping. You were aching to say that, weren't you, little one?"

"Perhaps I was. After all, I can take so much!"

He smiled briefly with his eyes: "You just remember what a brute I am when you meet Freedman again!"

Dazedly Andrea passed a hand over her eyes. "Let's get this over, shall we? I absolutely swear I'll behave. God knows what that involves – I've never looked sideways at the man!"

Steven's mocking, oblique glance was entirely unimpressed. He leaned forward and switched on the ignition, putting the jeep in gear and swinging back on to the track. Her eyes were drawn to his hands on the wheel, beautiful hands, really, lean and hard and strong. It came to her suddenly that Steven could be appallingly cruel!

Luke Freedman didn't fly in alone, as Andrea was quickly to find out. Even as she was changing her shirt and slacks for a cool filamel print, she could hear the crunch of the jeep's heavy tyres on the gravelled drive, the slam of doors, then the sound of voices carrying easily on the warm still air.

"Steven darling, it's wonderful to be back! You've no idea how I long for Mokhana when I'm in the city. The peace and the freedom!"

Andrea stood arrested, one hand uplifted, the sunlight glinting off the silver-backed hairbrush in her hand.

"I say, that's new, isn't it, darling?" the voice was asking, a throaty contralto, slightly drawling, superconfident. "The carriage lamp, I mean. A wonderful match for the glass panels – but then you always do get just what you've wanted!"

It was all Andrea could do not to rush to the window and lean far enough out to catch sight of the Voice. She could hear Steven's dark-timbred voice, the lighter tones of Dr. Freedman, then Helena Daintree's, dry, very clear, with an unprecedented vein of warmth and humour.

"Gillian, my dear! Dr. Freedman!" There was a short pause, presumably as Helena came down the stairs, perhaps to bestow a quick, dry kiss. "But what a surprise, Gillian," she continued. "And so welcome! Would you know I've just had a letter from your mother. From Geneva!"

"You're way behind the times, Aunt Helena," the bell tones were teasingly indulgent. "Mother's in Paris this week for the collections. She's a compulsive buyer, as we all know."

The rest of this fascinating dialogue was lost on Andrea as the voices receded into the interior of the hall. Andrea put down the brush, staring sightlessly at her own reflection. So Helena Daintree was capable of a friendly rapport with another woman! Somehow she found the fact vaguely incredible. Her eyes focused and she saw herself objectively as perhaps the owner of that ripe female voice would see her — a too-slender young girl, with a small boy's feathery hair-style, large-eyed, fine-featured, but with the soft, exquisite bloom of returning good health and vitality. She walked nearer the mirror. She wore no make-up beyond an iridescent pinky bronze lipstick, but then she rarely bothered to use any of the expensive cosmetics in the beauty case Steven had bought her. Her skin could pass the most critical muster even if she had the certain notion that the owner of that lush drawl would be the epitome of casual elegance. She hesitated for a moment, caught up with the idea of changing her dress for something a little more formal, then discarded the idea. She looked quite presentable with little variation from her normal day-to-day appearance.

When she got down to the living room, the womenfolk were already installed on the moiré-covered Empire sofa in the curve of the huge bay window. Helena Daintree looked up with a tolerant smile.

"Hello there, my dear. I've just been telling Gillian all about you. Come along in!" She turned to the soignée young woman beside her nursing a long frosted drink. "Gillian, my dear, may I introduce Andrea Swanson, our little house guest. Gillian Courtney, my dear, the daughter of my dearest friend!" She leaned over and patted the younger woman's hand. "At one time, Gillian dear, I had the highest hopes that your mother and Garth would make a match of it!"

"I'm very glad they *didn't*!" Gillian Courtney returned very smartly indeed, and both women shared a moment of amused comprehension.

Andrea returned the bright smile that was directed towards her, but neither girl extended a hand. Gillian Courtney wasn't a *girl* precisely, but a poised and knowing brunette in her late twenties, more striking than good-looking, very tall and ultra-elegant in black slacks and a matching, sleeveless jacket, with a white, tie-necked, long-sleeved crepe blouse underneath. Her satiny black hair was parted very severely in the centre and drawn back into a knot on the nape, gold hoop ear-rings in her ears.

Andrea let her eyes slip over the new arrival unobtrusively. As she had guessed, Gillian Courtney was meticulously made up – or "the whole bit", as Andrea put it to herself, noting the amber eye-shadow, the long sherry-coloured eyes carefully extended, the heavily mascaraed eyelashes, the golden sheen of a glossy see-through foundation, the thinnish lips artfully built up to a fuller outline. To a certain extent her looks were a miracle of make-up, but they were well worth the effort. Without being a

101

beauty, Gillian Courtney would undoubtedly turn heads.

The same sherry-coloured eyes were appraising Andrea with no such attempt at discretion, only the hard, clear, merchandising assessment one might expect of the daughter of a compulsive spender.

"And how are you feeling now, Miss Swanson?" Gillian Courtney was asking in the faintly bored tones she invariably kept for invalids.

Andrea was spared the necessity for answering as Luke Freedman came back into the room, followed at a distance by Steven.

"Andrea!" he exclaimed aloud, his eyes flashing as he caught sight of her.

She turned her head in relief and caught that unguarded expression, a curious mixture of pent-up longing and professional approval. She put out her hand, her soft, musical voice infused with feeling.

"Dr. Freedman, how very nice to see you again!"

He savoured her words, finding them far short of his own feelings, but he couldn't have asked for a more subtly illuminating smile. He moved forward quickly, just a little off balance, conscious of Daintree's ever-watchful aquamarine eyes, holding out both his hands.

She looked not unlike one of the creamy, blossoming lilies that graced the garden, he thought, his eyes on the bloom of her skin, the clear, lustrous eyes, the softest cloud grey. He supposed he had Daintree to thank for that. Certainly she looked "cherished". His own choice of words surprised him, but there was no doubt she had been well looked after. There was a faint gilding on her skin, in contrast to the silvery fairness of her hair. Sturm had worked a small miracle in keeping the flap clear of her forehead. There was no trace of her scar through the lengthening hair. He took her hand, holding it between his own, fighting down the mad impulse to gather her against him and kiss her.

"You look like a flower!" he said simply. "In fact I think I'm here under false pretences, you're so obviously well looked after!"

"Country charm, Doctor?" Gillian Courtney asked playfully. "We *are* here on another matter, however!"

Luke Freedman scarcely heard her, his eyes roaming over Andrea's face, her hand still caught up in his own. Then, as though realising he had held it over-long, he dropped it and turned back to his host.

"From her eyes and her good clear colour, I'd say she was going along fine. As Miss Courtney pointed out, it's as well we have this hospital venture under discussion."

"Naturally we must have *you* on the committee, Aunt Helena," Gillian Courtney interposed smoothly, spreading her capable hands. "I've got the most marvellous ideas worked out for fund-raising – some involving Mokhana!" She looked up suddenly at Steven, her long eyes heavy-lidded and languorous.

"I'll fall in with them, Gillian," he responded dryly. "There's no need for the witchcraft!"

"But I *like* it, darling," she said provocatively, still holding his eyes with her own, a sensual awareness emanating from her indolent body.

Helena Daintree looked on, faintly amused and indulgent. "I assume you're talking about the new wing?" she asked with a slight spasm of enthusiasm. "The Board are lucky to have your services, Gillian. You're a born organiser, dear!"

"I do what I can!" Gillian rejoined, not displeased by the appellation.

Helena Daintree smiled and rose gracefully to her feet.

"I'll go see Sammy about lunch. I know Dr. Freedman has to be back at the hospital by tomorrow, but how long can you spare us, Gillian?"

"Till I'm *thrown* out!" Gillian Courtney said with extravagant gaiety and the easy confidence of one who was sure of their popularity.

"And *that* will be never!" Helena Daintree assured her, transferring her dark-eyed gaze to Luke Freedman. "Doctor, if you'd like to speak to Andrea privately, there's the small sitting-room off the sun-porch. Andrea will show you where. Excuse me, won't you? I'll get Sammy to prepare a seafood cocktail. I know how Gillian loves them, and the king prawns from the Gulf have never been better!"

Gillian Courtney sighed voluptuously and linked her hands behind her head, drawing the crepe tight over the well-moulded breasts.

"How you spoil me, Auntie dear!" She slanted a narrow-eyed glance at Steven, as dark and enigmatic as ever. "Come and sit beside me, darling. I've so much to tell you, and you *did* promise to let me have Mokhana!"

"For a *week-end*!" he pointed out suavely, but he did lower his long lithe frame to the sofa beside her, his shapely mouth faintly indulgent, as his aunt's had been. The whole room was suddenly charged with new forces; a realignment into camps.

"Now's as good a time as ever for a routine check-up, Andrea," Luke Freedman said easily. "Heart, blood pressure, reflexes, no more!" He took Andrea's elbow. "Come along and fill me in with your progress. No more headaches, no visual disturbances . . . anything like that?"

They walked out into the hallway where Luke paused to pick up his bag, not hearing Gillian's faintly malicious comment:

"The doctor's rather a *case*, isn't he? Of course she *is* rather lovely in a white, virginal sort of way. But seriously, darling, why play games with me!"

CHAPTER VI

FOR the first time since she had come to Mokhana, Andrea spent a long time dressing for dinner, applying make-up with a hand she soon found was both light and expert, stepping carefully into her dress and zipping the low back. Finally she stood away from the mirror and subjected herself to an intense, self-forgetful scrutiny. She was rather dazed by what she saw! Once or twice, in a careless, offhand fashion, Steven had called her beautiful, but she never thought of herself as that. Tonight she was different — a stranger, with a lovely, excitement-touched face, wide, luminous eyes, softly shaded, a shining aureole of hair, gently coaxed into height and body, the singing perfection of her slender body sheafed in one of the long, sheer dacron dresses Steven had bought for her.

The tiny, deeply oval bodice was sheer white, with cut-away shoulders, and tiny covered buttons to the narrow waist, the floating skirt a swirling cloud pattern of pearl grey and white. It was a beautiful dress and it might have been designed exclusively with her in mind. It was a warm, tropic night of ripe moon and the tall palms in the garden swaying. It had already gone seven! She moved under the sparkling cascade of the bedroom chandelier with its hundred and one prisms and it touched her hair with a transient glory before she flicked the switch and threw the room into a melting, black darkness.

Her part of the house was only faintly lit, assuming no definite shape, only a deep amber glow, stealthy and mysterious. She would turn on a few lights as she passed.

She slipped along the passageway with noiseless feet, coming to a halt as a long shadow fell across the top of the stairway. It was Steven. He paused, unaware of her, putting up a hand to flick on a light switch. Her heart lunged at the sudden radiance on his dark, handsome face. Her presence must have penetrated his consciousness, for he turned his head sharply and flung a rapier glance along the passageway.

"Andrea?"

She went forward into the pool of light, grave now, staring up at him. His head was thrown back, his eyes gleaming, the light glancing off his high cheekbones, a vertical fold between his slanting dark brows, heightening his saturnine expression. There was, unaccountably, a tension between them that could not be imagined out of existence. A muscle tautened beside his hard, imperious mouth, his strange eyes raked her mercilessly.

"Girl into swan!"

Her own expression changed elusively while she sought to find words adequate to express what she was feeling.

"Obviously my appearance doesn't please you!" The light threw shadowed hollows into her cheeks, a bloom over her skin, a silver nimbus around her head.

His glance sharpened, a biting sardonic inflection in his voice.

"Whatever gave you *that* insane notion? I'm sure you're more than most men could hope for in a lifetime. Most certainly Freedman!"

A dark glitter of antagonism spun out between them. She drew a quick little breath like a tortured child. "Oh, please, Steven, I had no thought of dressing to please anyone!" *Unless it was you* unspoken, the words lurched in her. "Your aunt made a point of telling me we would be dressing for dinner. You have, yourself!" She could scarcely bear to glance at the beautiful cut and cloth of his jacket.

"I would have thought a girl with your assets didn't need to go to so much bother!" His voice was toneless, the very tonelessness unnatural, accentuating her feeling of being whirled into danger. With the light behind him he looked oddly untameable, quite capable of anything, strange leaping lights in the depths of his eyes.

Her head was slightly bent, her lashes thick and heavy on her cheeks, her tender nape exposed to his sight.

"I might remind you, Steven, *you* bought this dress. If you find it overdone, you might blame yourself!"

"What a ridiculous suggestion!" he said with arrogant simplicity. "I'm quite sure of my own taste."

"Then why do you like hurting me?" She tilted her head briefly, almost defiantly.

"Why do *you* think?" There was a wholly masculine appraisal on his face. "Perhaps you're the kind of woman a man likes to hurt for the sheer pleasure of kissing her better!"

"I can't see you adopting so drastic a measure!" she said with soft irony. "Surely Gillian is more to your taste? Much more rewarding to make love to!"

"Did I say I've made love to her?" he demanded very evenly, his eyes narrowing.

"But you *have*, haven't you?" She gave a shaky, bitter sweet little laugh.

His eyes gleamed, pinning her gaze in this cruel cat-and-the-mouse game. "I rarely discuss my affairs with schoolgirls, but the answer is, *yes*! Countless times. Believe me, she's nothing like you. She knows the score – an unfailing help in an adult situation!"

He was effectively barring her way and she pushed his arm aside. "You beast!" She tried to hold herself in under her pounding blood, but all that splendid dark insolence was too much for her, a lick of flame towards dynamite. His arm tautened to steel and she pushed futilely against it, her heart pounding erratically. "Let me past, Steven!"

He imprisoned her wrist, holding it implacably but not hurting it.

"Who's giving orders in my own house? Up to date, little one, I've been handling you like Meissen china."

He was too tall, too powerful, too able to reduce all her struggles to impotence. "Don't think I don't know what's behind all that smooth urbanity," she said tightly. "You've a devil in you, Steven!"

His soft laughter touched her curls. "Well, be warned then, you foolish child. Don't tempt the fall of fire!" A dark, sardonic humour leapt in his eyes. "I might have known all that coolness was only a pretence. Fire and ice is rather a dangerous combination for a woman to possess. So unexpected and *so* unsettling!"

Andrea shut her eyes, swaying slightly, and he drew her back hard against him, his hands at her narrow waist, the tips of his fingers touching the slight bones of her hips. She turned her head along his hard chest, lost in the terrible meaning of what he meant to her. His hands moved and tightened around her rib-cage, his voice deliberately tantalising.

"Open your eyes, Andrea!"

They were facing a long mirrored panel set into the wall and she caught their arrested reflection. Colour flooded her face, a monumental panic at her own transparency, her inability to conceal her own needs, her mouth still curved with unconscious, wild longings.

"Answer me now," he said tautly. "Are you fighting to get *away* from me or what?"

She looked very pale and fragile against his lean, dark

strength, her bare shoulders gleaming against the sombre cloth of his jacket. His hands shifted to the sides of her neck, holding her head up.

"Well?"

She made a queer little sound, her fears for herself entirely forgotten.

"I said it would be easy to hate you, Steven, but I never guessed *how* easy!" She looked beautiful and intense, a fire inside her, aroused to a reckless passion, the colour swimming into her cheeks, lightening her eyes to a silvery sparkle.

He only laughed, looking extraordinarily dominant and vital.

"Youthful agonies are the same the world over. You're no different, little one. But don't provoke a scene *now*," he said softly, "or I might have to carry you somewhere they might never find us again. In this house it could be done!"

She was trembling, her great eyes lifted to his, icy with fury.

"Touch me and I'll scream! I *can*, you know," she boasted, "although I've been over-long in finding my voice. I owe you that much, I suppose, for saving my life!"

"You owe me *nothing*!" His hand shot out and encircled her wrist, but her voice played a queer trick on her and died in her throat.

"Maybe an emotional upheaval is just what you need," he said with peculiar quiet, "but not tonight!" His voice slowed to a pleasant drawl as though there had never been a suspicion of anger or antagonism between them. "Come along, Andrea, I've only been pretending indifference to your appearance. You're an exquisite child – but such a temper! You might have warned me and I could have left you in the forest!" He drew her along with him, his thumb moving over the veins in her wrist. "And just by way of a reward," he added conversationally, "I have a little something that might go with your dress. I didn't quite realise you'd be needing jewellery quite so quickly, but then, we've never had visitors before!" he drawled insolently his glittery gaze slanting in winged satire over her face and bare shoulders.

Her fingers clenched convulsively in his, but he only laughed beneath his breath, straightening them out against his palm. "I've almost got it in my heart to feel *sorry* for Freedman," he added dryly.

They were at dinner at last – Chinese style, in Gillian's honour, each course as delicious as it was exotic, its preparation not without incident in the kitchen, for Sammy, under professional stress, was anything but imperturbable. Netta, in a spotless blue uniform, circled the table like a winging bird, serving the deep-fried shrimps with a crystal glaze and set in a bed of lettuce; the steaming mounds of fried rice and fried noodles, shredded pork and chicken balls with green peppers, bamboo shoots and steamed vegetables, and to follow, apple fritters, Chinese style, with a wonderfully brittle toffee coating, her merry black eyes disapproving of Andrea's small portions.

"Marvellous!" Gillian, something of a gourmet, waited until Steven had refilled her wine glass, then twirled it idly, admiring the light golden Riesling with its tinge of green, then she smiled over its crystal rim. "Sammy, I mean," she enthused. "He's a fabulous cook, a capacity I find completely terrifying myself!"

Steven was looking at her with coolly amused detachment, but a deep beguiling note thread his voice. "I doubt if you're a good sample of domesticity, Gill!"

"But terribly modern, darling!" She slanted her eyes at him, her body curved towards him. "You must grant me that, barring the usual feminist programme, though sometimes I think I might have done better in a naughtier age – the gay nineties, perhaps?"

Apparently unaffected, he raised his brows. "Instead of which, as a result of a life of complete indolence, you've turned your hand to charitable works!"

"Always supposing they don't turn out complete flops, wouldn't you say, Dr. Freedman?" She flickered a brief glance at the other man, then returned her attention to Steven like a homing bird. "Honestly, Steven, I adore you! You don't really think Nature intended me to boil eggs, and darn socks, childbirth in a cyclone, that sort of thing! Indolent, indeed! Like you've been keeping records. At any rate, you're *exactly* as usual!"

He saluted her with his wineglass. "I'm very gratified to hear it!"

"Brute!" she made a provocative little moue with her mouth, "even if you are the man I've dreamed about all my life, and so horribly rich! The most enviable situation there is!"

"On the contrary, it *isn't*," he said dryly, "and I don't mind admitting it!"

"You certainly should," she said blithely, and reached out a fingertip to trail it innocently but suggestively along his palm. "What you really need is a *wife*! After all, a man can't possibly get reckless with his money without one!" Her long, mascaraed lashes veiled a look of burning steadiness. She sat back with a gay, appealing gesture. "There now, I've been wanting to say that for a long time!"

"To my certain knowledge you said it the *last* time you

111

were here!" Steven returned suavely, his teeth very white in the polished teak of his face. His aunt, smiling and indulgent, in a Renaissance-type gown, threw up her hands.

"Steven darling, don't tease! I'm sure Gillian's right!" She presided at the opposite end of the table to Steven, very relaxed and unguarded, and Andrea put it down to Gillian's presence. She was mildly amused to see Luke Freedman studying Gillian with puzzled interest, almost like a new species under the microscope, until Gillian returned his gaze thoughtfully and he dropped his eyelids and looked away, colouring faintly at Andrea's faint smile of comprehension.

Gillian continued to effervesce, holding Steven's palm like a clairvoyant. "You will make love to many women but love only one," she said seductively, "and you will marry her and be wonderfully happy!"

"In spite of my emotional lacerations?" he inquired sardonically, his eyes sliding over Andrea's light gilded face. "While you're there you don't happen to see a tall brunette, I suppose?"

Gillian threw his hand away. "My darling Steven, that's giving the game away. But honestly, the happiness line is very, very strong, in spite of all these so-called lacerations. You bear your scars well!"

"Don't I have to!" he countered dryly.

"I don't suppose you would care to read mine?" Luke Freedman asked with faintly sarcastic good humour.

"I'd be delighted, Doctor." Gillian turned to slide her eyes over the other man. "It's Blossom Moon, you know!" Her eyes widened blatantly. "Don't you ever consider marriage, Doctor?"

"Often!" he smiled to himself, thinking, just lately, *how* often.

"And *you*, Steven, if you're to be believed at all?"

"*Never!*" he cut her off with relaxed insolence. "Not even in my wildest flights of passion."

Well, you couldn't ask for anything plainer than that! Andrea thought, and avoided his shockingly brilliant eyes. Gillian, however, was plainly not to be put off, and her white coral ear-rings swung against her dark golden face.

"You should, darling! " she mewed plaintively. "Even a caged tiger can learn to be contented! "

He turned towards her and made a little mocking noise. "Drop it, Gill, or the whole evening will be flawed."

She touched his hand lightly. "If you insist, darling. You're so self-sufficient, it frightens me! "

She didn't look in the least frightened, Andrea thought, but in undisputed possession of the dinner table, needing no other than Steven to carry the burden of talk, her gestures broad yet graceful, her indigo black hair as severely dressed as before, looking very dramatic in a flowing long gown of silk jersey with gorgeous colour combinations. Netta came in with coffee and Andrea sipped at hers gratefully, admiring the exquisite little porcelain cup.

All through dinner Gillian's voice had beaten on her eardrums like a veritable opera with exchanges that were quite lost on her, at least – references to tiresome people, lovely people, the peculiar awfulness of a mutual friend, the hectic round of parties coming up, her mother's latest romance with an Italian Count, or at least he *said* he was a Count and he *did* have lovely manners. She was witty, she was malicious, she was often inconsequential, but from under her lashes, Andrea was forced to concede that Gillian was holding Steven's attention, with his aunt, plainly gratified, looking on. Irrationally, she felt wounded, not realising, at first, that she was suffering the

113

first agonising thrusts of sexual jealousy. As though conscious of her regard, Gillian shot her a sharp look of inquiry, considerably irked by the way the light seemed trapped in those silvery curls, lingering on the highly caressable line of a bare shoulder, the pure grace from forehead to chin to throat, realising with a pang that helpless fragility had a witching effect on some men. It might pay to get the girl moving. With this idea in mind she said vigorously:

"I suppose you wouldn't care to give us a hand on the committee, Miss Swanson. Nothing very active, of course. A little typing, sending out invitations, that sort of thing?"

Before Andrea even had the opportunity of formulating an answer Steven intervened dryly:

"A for effort, Gill, but nothing doing. Andrea's not up to it at the moment. I'm sure there are any number of high-minded society females you could fall back on!"

"But of course, *skillions*, darling!" Gillian gave a throaty, three-noted laugh curiously devoid of amusement, giving rise to a faint tension in Luke Freedman. He turned to smile at Andrea, to find her fine eyes tilted at the corners lingering in his, some of her reserve melting away. She had been charmingly polite to him, but she was undoubtedly withdrawn, a little isolated, animated yet dreamy, forbiddingly lovely in the soft pool of light that made an island of the dinner table. Trust Daintree to squash the committee idea! It would have given him some excuse to see her. Outwardly Daintree appeared to be paying little attention to Andrea, yet he watched her all the time. A strange man, Daintree, he reflected – cultivated, cosmopolitan, but with something inexplicable about him, for all the striking intensity of those aquamarine eyes. Gillian Courtney, for her part, seemed totally absorbed in the man, looking at him, devouring him, the quality of her glance so intense, so secretly excited, a reddish glow in her sherry-coloured eyes. Perhaps they would make a match of it. Gillian Courtney had style and distinction of a sort and she was, undoubtedly, a tryer.

Beside him Andrea wasn't aware that she was staring into space, her eyes wide and luminous, registering the scene on her inner eyes, one hand playing with the lovely bauble at her throat, a large, perfect Coral Sea pearl, on a fine gold chain, that fell to the shadowed cleft of her breast.

"Andrea, my dear, where have you gone to?" Helena Daintree gave a faint laugh, her eyes like an inquisitor's on the pearl at the girl's throat.

"Don't tease the poor child!" Gillian said protectively. "After all, it's not every day Steven gets ignored!"

Andrea blinked her lashes slowly. "I implore you to forgive me!"

Steven's eyes narrowed over her, gleaming like a cat's. "That's quite all right, little one, I know you can't help it. I merely said it's Blossom Moon. Gillian has been asking about all the chanting that's going on. Would you care to see a corroboree?"

To have smiled at him would have required an effort of will that was quite beyond her. He seemed skilled at using his voice as a fine instrument to draw on emotion at will. No doubt he found her an easy target, with this odd, restless excitement shifting through her veins. A cool indifference registered in her eyes.

"Yes, I would!" she said briefly.

"No one's *forcing* you, little one!" he said, his smile sharpening.

Her delicate hands lay in her lap, her huge eyes, for once, unfathomable. "But I'd *like* to, Steven," she spoke

115

with silky distinctness. "They're actually the plainest words I can find!"

Something feline and elemental in her warmed to the sudden fire in his eyes. There was swiftly, too swiftly, a subtle antagonism between them. "With *some* women," he drawled conversationally, "you never know where you are! So charming, so natural, so utterly false!"

"Oh, come on now, Steven," Gillian joined in with exquisite ease. "Next you'll be telling us we have no principles!"

"Not at all!" He turned on her with hard, mocking charm. "No *masculine* ones, at any rate!"

"Foiled!" she said laconically, and made a little moue of indignation. "How do you know we're not hoarding up all these little insults?"

"*Are* you, little one?" Steven turned to Andrea with careless confidence. "It's about time to call your bluff!"

"Indeed I am," she said lightly, her eyes shimmering like ice crystals. "I'm mortally hurt, though it's my certain conviction all men are villains at heart!"

Luke Freedman turned towards her with mock horror. "You can't believe that, Andrea?"

"With one or two exceptions," she amended, smiling at him with her eyes and her mouth, so that it seemed to him he could never get tired of looking into her face.

Steven shot back his cuff and looked down at his wristwatch. "It will take us about an hour to come down on the old tribal grounds. Are you coming, Helena?"

"No, thank you, dear." Helena Daintree signalled Netta for more coffee. "Gillian has brought me all the latest glossies, so I'll just have a lazy time here."

"Well then, if you'll excuse us, the girls will have to change their dresses. We might have a bit of scrambling to do to find a good position." He stood up and held Gil-

116

lian's chair. She rose gracefully and swivelled around to face him.

"I'm a passionate nature-worshipper myself! " Her sherry-coloured eyes seemed unable to withdraw from his mouth.

"From *afar*! " he commented with irony.

She brushed his chin with her hand. "Don't bother me with unimportant distinctions, darling. It's too glorious a night to stay indoors anyway! "

Luke Freedman smiled down on Andrea's elegant small head. "I can't help but agree with that! "

"Yes, indeed, this promises to be rather *amusing*," Gillian drawled, her eyes on Luke Freedman's absorbed face, a flicker of sardonic humour around her wide, shapely mouth.

"A word so incongruous, I'm forced into noticing it! " Steven said shortly, and moved towards the door with his peculiar lithe tread.

"Forgive my lack of dignity, darling." Gillian hurried after him, her long skirt moulding her smooth thighs. "It's so difficult to attempt a defence when there's none possible! "

It was a night of full moon and *magrada*. Love chants rose on the night wind, gathered to a crescendo, then faded into an eerie silence, the air alive with persistent beats of the spirit drums, never varying in rhythm and tone, echoing miles away to the sleeping ranges, making the skin prickle with a primitive excitement. Into this cachophony slipped the tap-sticks, clear and sharp, the chitter-chatter of sacred stones, the deep, weird notes of the didgeridoo, the drone pipe.

To Andrea, the night sky of Mokhana appeared like a dream pavilion with Oongra, the Moon God, throwing a

117

net of gold over the open savannahs, deep silent shadows into the mysterious wooded thickets, heavy with blossom and scent, queer little rustlings. Above them, the Milky Way was a spangled ribbon flung like a jewelled belt from the Guiding Light, the Southern Cross, to the boundaries of the western meridian. Somewhere many miles from the house, an ancient dance festival was being staged, dedicated to the sacred spirit totems of the Emu and Eagle-hawk tribes. The plaintive love chants persisted on the breeze, coming strongly now, tuneless to a degree, but with a definite emotional scale.

In the back of the jeep Andrea lifted her face to the night wind, finding the radiant landscape unutterably lovely. She gave a sigh of pleasure and Luke Freedman looked down at her shining head.

"Quite a night, isn't it?" he murmured with laconic understatement. "No wonder at all the tribes worship the Sky People! Look at the moon – limpid as a pool of gold. Outsize stars, low enough to touch them. There's one shooting. Make a wish, Andrea!"

An easy companionship spun like a charm between them. "I already have!" she smiled, turning up her face. She seemed to be looking through and beyond him with such a quality of mystery and magic that his senses stirred, almost a kind of drunkenness, he thought half ironically. Yet he was solaced by the reality of her by his side, each minute precious and spinning by so fast. He had lived with the memory of her day and night, a memory that intruded into his working hours despite all his efforts to shut her out.

"May I ask what it was?" he asked, his voice was gentle as a caress.

"To recapture the past. And no more!"

Immediately his smile vanished. "You will, Andrea,

118

I'm sure. It's not so very long ago that your life hung in the balance. You're doing wonderfully well as you are!"

"I'm not complaining," she said quickly. "It's just a curious feeling to live in a vacuum!"

"I know, but there you are!" he said rather helplessly, at a loss to offer any more. It must indeed be a curious feeling and she was acting with dignity and courage.

Gillian's heavy raillery came as a shock to both of them. She turned her sleek head over her shoulder.

"Stop whispering, you two!"

"I didn't realise we *were*, especially!" Luke said in that calm way of his.

Gillian's mocking laugh plainly dubbed him a liar, but Steven said nothing at all, driving very fast, his profile gilded by the moonlight, throwing into relief the dark sculpture of his head. He was making towards the sound of the woman chant, faintly melancholy, now gay, its origin older than the Pyramids. It seemed to be coming from the direction of the blue lily lagoon, once sacred ground. The wind rushed through the tall paperbarks, scattering blossom, and Steven pulled the jeep into the night-time jungle of a giant banyan tree with its multiple prop roots and bark carving forty feet up.

The spirit drums were everywhere now, speaking to the night. Thrumba! thrumba! thrumba! thrum! their very insistence making a tumult in the blood. Gillian seemed especially affected, her eyes half glazed, caught up in the primeval spell of the night and the dance.

"We'll make it on foot from now on," Steven said in an undertone. "Just keep behind me. I know the track like the back of my hand." His gaze slid over Andrea's head, spun silver as she moved out into full moonlight. "You could have done with a head-scarf, little one. Your hair is like a banner. I don't particularly want to *advertise*

119

our presence."

"Here, use this!" Gillian unwound the navy and emerald bandana she wore at her throat, thrusting it into Andrea's hand with careless good nature.

Andrea took the scarf with a quick "thank you" and twirled it swiftly around her head, tying the ends.

"Ready now?" Steven was anxious to move off, moving lithely, with swinging grace, hard and contained. "Luke, you might keep Andrea in front of you. It's not all easy going to get to a vantage point."

"As good as done!" Luke responded easily, his blue eyes exploring the fine contours of Andrea's face, offset by the tight, dark head-scarf.

Several times on their way down to the quicksilver sheet of water, Andrea had cause to be grateful for his every-ready hand, helping her over the worst bits, padding softly on, weaving this way and that, holding branches back for her, pausing to let her regain her breath. On the crest of a slope thick with couch grass, they looked down on the lagoon, heavily fringed on the far side by thick vegetation, kapoks and casuarinas, pandanus and paperbarks. A circle of fires ringed the gravelly sands, tendered by young lubras with plump piccaninnies, tousle-haired and intensely curious, by their side. In the dancing flames, lithe bodies, ochre-dabbed, red, white and yellow, moved with deep, ritualistic grace to the leaping flames, welcoming in the blossom moon and the flower people, the spirit folk who hovered, invisibly, beyond the circle of flame.

The women moved gracefully through the lines of male dancers, their black eyes shining below a fringe of bloodwood seeds. They were the blossoms, the butterflies, the birds and the bees, picturesque and remarkably clear in their symbolic movements. The drums and the tap-sticks beat out a firm, lively rhythm with radiant cries of excitement from the coffee-hued faces of the spectators who threw kindling on the fires. The night was stirring with the urgency of their beat. It was a strangely moving experience, shadow figures from the Dreamtime, struggling for existence in the white man's world, striving from long ages past to preserve the race.

It was, as Steven explained, barely above a whisper, an entertainment corroboree to which women were permitted to be present, and even take part in, as opposed to the sacred rituals from which women were rigidly excluded, the rites and traditions of the tribes, like more civilised cultures, being solely vested in the male.

New chants broke out every minute or so with a curiously nasal intonation, rising, then falling, then dying away. The dancers broke ranks, then a new chant was intoned, powerful in attack, throbbing with a barbaric sound. Dusky-skinned lubras, clattering woomeras, their bodies burnished with goanna oil, religiously tended the holy fires, their lips moving soundlessly, for they were not permitted to chant aloud, the stamp of their feet and their hisses accentuating the stresses of the chant.

The grass tufts tickling her chin, Andrea felt Luke's gaze upon her. "It's rather awesome, isn't it?" she whispered, genuinely unsettled.

He smiled and patted her hand. "This is supposed to be an entertainment. Now if you're talking about initiation and hunt corroborees, they just could be awesome!"

"This is quite enough for me!" she returned feelingly with a smile that betrayed a measure of relief. The whole staging and execution of the dance, naturalistically brilliant, still held her as taut as a bowstring.

For an hour they watched the motions of the dance, working now towards a fever pitch of excitement, then

Steven, catching sight of her tense small face, gave the signal to leave, moving back towards the column of trees with all the lithe grace of a cat. His eyes seemed to gleam faintly iridescent, his hand on the soft flesh of Gillian's upper arm, able to bestow at will the gift of sensual excitement. She had her face upturned to him, on her mouth a queerly satisfied smile, akin to a languorous complaisance.

Andrea studied them for a moment, thoughtfully narrowing her eyes, envisaging a possibility she was beginning to dread. The spirit of the mysterious night seemed in control of her feet. She was flying along easily following Luke's lead, smiling gently at his little whispered comments, grateful for the warm touch of his hand, trying not to analyse the special look in his eyes. The wind-blown palms, the whispering of the leaves, all had a message, inducing a certain unwariness. Under the thick canopy of trees, their leafy arms interlocked in a parasitic embrace, they moved quickly and in silence began to climb again.

Half way across the inky blackness of the thicket Andrea felt a sharp twinge on her head-scarf as it sailed back with the quick release of a branch.

"Damn! damn! damn!" She came to a quick stop knowing a moment of confused panic. Had it been her own scarf she would gladly have left it to an inquisitive lorikeet, but it would have to be Gillian's. She couldn't afford to lose it. She spun on her heel and looked back along the dense grove, her eyes frantically trying to pierce the gloom. It had to be somewhere close at hand. She had a split second to find it. Luke, quite unconscious of her predicament, was surging ahead.

"Andrea?" On the crest of the rise he slid urgently back, swearing in emotional haste.

122

"What in God's name is wrong?" Daintree swerved violently, alerted to that harsh note of panic.

"It's Andrea!" Luke said, his voice sharp with anxiety, cursing the way Daintreee had of throwing him off balance. "One minute she was here, right beside me. Now she's gone!"

Eyes narrowed, intensely alert, Daintree moved back to him. "All that matters now is where the devil is she?"

"I'm a hell of a scout!" Luke muttered with a discernible note of self-disgust.

Daintree didn't bother to deny it. He appeared in complete control of himself. "Keep on going to the jeep. Take Gillian. I'll go back for Andrea. She can't be too far away. She's missed her way through the trees." He didn't wait to see them move off, but disappeared into the murky blackness, as silent and purposeful as any big cat.

The thicket had a tangible presence that drained her of confidence. It was stupid to be frightened, but she was. Ever since her experience in the rain jungle, unrelieved darkness was an intolerable burden, awakening in her an overwhelming surge of loneliness and unease. It was a brooding darkness, and she was lost in it, growing nervier and nervier. She drew a deep breath and tried to relax herself, but the sound of the spirit drums and the quick rustlings in the undergrowth made that impossible. All the living beauty of the night had gone!

A firefly, green with ghostly light, floated past her and she hit out at it wildly with a terror not of darkness but of unseen things, a primitive fear, engendered by the unsettling effect of the corroboree. She was abandoned, all alone, yet not alone. Steven would come for her, taut and glitter-eyed, angered at her foolishness in losing sight of the rest of them. There was a sudden swishing of branches, the crackling of footsteps on the dry bracken.

She swallowed dryly, unable to find her voice, doubting the wisdom of finding it just at that moment.

"Andrea?"

It was Steven. His voice had an imperative quality, a hard note of anxiety, a faint edge of violence.

"I'm here!" Her voice broke in almost hysterical reaction. "Over here. I lost you!"

He followed her voice, a travesty of itself, soft and shaken, verging on tears. He was upon her almost before she could distinguish his tall frame, reaching out for her, his hands closing over the delicate bones of her shoulders. At once, his relief turned to a sparkling jet of anger.

"God!" he burst out wrathfully, "if this sort of thing keeps up, I'll have to chain you to my wrist!"

She swayed towards him in an aching need for comfort. "Hold me, Steven. Just hold me, don't rage!"

His breath sizzled her ear. "*Hold* you?" His voice held an odd element, dropping to a dark undertone. "Yes, I'll hold you. Hold you, thrash you, it's all the same!" But his voice and his hands were at conflict, for he encircled her slight body, folding her against him with exquisite strength, letting her draw on the radiant energy that was so much a part of him.

She closed her eyes with a drugged sort of rapture, crushing her face up against his soft shirt, hearing the thud of his heart.

"You're palpitating like a spent bird!" he murmured, his chiselled mouth touching her hair. "What was it?"

"The trees, I think!" she said shakily, a tension coming back into her throat. "The darkness closing in on me. It reminded me a little of the rain forest!"

"Little fool!" he muttered, drawing her still closer into that protective embrace. "Stop trembling. I'll have you out of here in no time! "

But his nearness was already evoking a wild sweet madness that had to be overcome. She stirred against him and immediately he released her, keeping an iron arm along her back. "How in hell Freedman ever lost track of you, I'll never know! " he said brusquely.

"It wasn't Luke's fault! " she protested. "Not at all. I should have called out to him, but I thought it would only take a minute. I lost Gillian's head-scarf. It's still around here somewhere! "

His voice tautened to hard impatience. "The devil take Gillian's scarf! It's easily replaced. What a foolish child you are, Andrea. Next time, if there *is* another next time, I'll keep you right under my arm. That way I'll save time having to go back for you. Now let's get back to the house. You could do with a tot of brandy. It won't hurt you and it might settle all those tremors you can't control! "

They had reached the jeep in a wordless silence; once out into the grasslands, the going was easy. Neither made an attempt to sit in the jeep but took up positions alongside. Gillian was stroking back her hair, fuming and fretting at his unexpected development, her eyes shadowed with the intensity of her feelings, her languor transmuted to a sharp irritability. With a vicious snap of her teeth she turned on Freedman uncontrollably.

"Couldn't you have kept a closer watch on the girl, knowing she's so damned helpless? This is a hellish thing to happen. It's damned well ruined my evening! "

The needling note in her voice really got to him. He turned on her a stare bright with hostility, alien to his nature.

"Are you trying to lecture me, Miss Courtney? I might
125

remind you, it's easy to *talk*!"

His protest left her cold and indifferent. "Oh, come off it, Doctor," she said with thinly veiled contempt. "Don't strike attitudes. This whole damned situation is getting out of hand, and you know it!"

"On the contrary, I don't follow you at all," he said with icy politeness.

"Have it your own way!" she said with weary impatience. "*You* may be content to bury your head in the sand, but I'm *not*. Helena was right! That girl is fast developing a dependence on Steven, that can't be allowed!"

"Why can't it?" he goaded her. "It's a temporary thing, after all. You might have a little charity – or is that too much to expect?"

"Oh, be your age!" she said crudely. "What I feel for Steven sweeps all other considerations aside. That girl has to go. And you're just the one to help her along!"

His expression froze into disdain. "I'd do nothing to jeopardise Andrea's wellbeing," he said curtly.

"Don't I know it!" her voice openly mocked him. "But if you think about it, Doctor, you'll realise it's for her own good. I don't have to spell it out, surely? I want Steven Daintree and I've got a better chance than anyone of getting him. Don't think I've devoted the best part of ten years all for nothing. I can't have that girl underfoot, but *you* . . ." her expression hardened to cynicism, "you could well do with her. I'm not blind, you know!"

His voice sprang its leash of tight self-control. "I don't think for one moment you are, Miss Courtney. Neither was I fooled by your cadging a ride out here."

She gave a laugh of genuine amusement. "Never leave anything to chance – that's my motto, Doctor, the only one if you want to succeed in this world. Helena acquainted me with the facts, so I hightailed it out here by the first possible plane – yours, as it happened. And I *am* helping on your damned committee, you know!"

"Women, my God!" he shook his head. "How devious can you get? What a lovely surprise, Gillian!" he cruelly mimicked Helena Daintree's dry, precise tones.

She smiled darkly as if relishing some inner joy. "Well, it *was* a lovely surprise to read all she had to say in her letter."

It came to him suddenly that he disliked her intensely. "I suppose congratulations are in order. You have a powerful ally. I wouldn't care to spend the rest of my days sharing a house with the woman, myself!"

"How naïve can you get!" Her voice was lush and rounded, supremely self-assured. "Believe me, Doctor, when I become Mrs. Steven Daintree, our Helena will be the first to go!"

"Well, well, well!" The glance he directed on her was almost devoid of expression, surprise even. "One never stops learning in a lifetime. And I thought you were devoted accomplices!"

She shook her head in reproof of this stupid assumption. "I learned very early, like my dear mamma before me, it's much better to make a friend of Helena Daintree than an enemy. It's easy to butter her up if you know how. But I won't stand by and let her ruin *my* marriage!"

"Like Vivienne Daintree?" he asked with a flash of perception.

"*Exactly!*" The word and the underlying sentiment was very distinct. "According to Mamma she gave Vivienne hell! Apparently Vivienne was one of those high-minded, imaginative girls you sometimes come across, soft enough to be practically liquid. At any rate, she never complained, never forced a ding-dong row. Just let

Helena jostle her out of the number one position, to the point where she thought her sister-in-law was more important to her husband and son than she was."

"Wretched woman!" In the moonlight Luke's face appeared to bleach under pressure.

"She's that!" Gillian agreed dryly. "Faint wonder I want her *out*. But until I'm Mrs. Daintree, I can wait!"

"You'll have a job on your hands!" His glance was half taunt, half irony.

"I think not!" her self-confidence was unshakeable. "I'm a lot younger than she is and quite as ruthless when it comes to getting what I want. Besides, Steven is not the man his father was. He's far more sensitive and imaginative."

He muffled a faint exclamation. "He strikes me as a chip off the old block!"

"But then you don't really know him, do you, Doctor?" She tilted her head, fastening her eyes on him. "Steven adored his mother, you know, although his father claimed nearly all his time, he was so proud of him. But Steven took it very hard when his mother cleared off and left them. He bottled it all up, fed on a constant diet of lies by his dear, loving aunt. Though God knows she *does* love him in her own peculiar way!"

"God!" In the radius of her company Luke's spine prickled. Andrea would be torn to pieces by these two hellcats.

"I don't know why I'm baring my soul like this!" Gillian gave a husky little chuckle. "I've never done so before. One starts out and inevitably tends to overdo it!"

"Perhaps you have been a little indiscreet!" he agreed waspishly, deriving a certain satisfaction from it.

Her eyes narrowed to reddish brown coals. "Oh, I don't know! I'd trust you with any secret, Doctor. You have that type of face."

"Don't trust me too far," he warned her. "I'm on Andrea's side, you know! You others can do as you like!"

"Precisely!" She jerked around, dislike on her mouth. "The very point I'm getting at. With any luck at all, I'll be Mrs. Steven Daintree by the end of the year."

"It would seem rather an ambitious plan," he observed with sarcasm.

"Leave that part of it to me. Just get the girl moving. She looks well enough to me. If it's money she'll be needing I daresay I could rake some up without Steven knowing."

For a second he was too astounded to speak, then he snapped at her:

"I don't think that will be at all necessary, Miss Courtney. I don't care to discuss Andrea in this way."

"It's a very high horse you're on, Doctor," she pointed out with malicious humour. "Careful you don't fall off!"

"You're very considerate all of a sudden!"

Her eyes gleamed impatiently. "Just remember I could talk to the girl myself, but I prefer to avoid unpleasantness, when I can. It's up to you, Doctor. Take it or leave it."

"And that's where you're wrong!" he said quietly, achieving a considerable degree of control. "It's up to Andrea. And here they come now. You might remember, yourself, that Daintree is strangely protective of her, though I don't suppose he realises it himself!"

They fell silent, tense and wary, as Steven and Andrea broke through the shadows of the trees into the brilliant moonlight.

CHAPTER VII

Her sleep that night was disturbed by wild, fragmentary dreams that left her listless and despondent – so much so that she came wide awake in the first rays of dawn almost at her farthest limit, fighting down nameless fears and anxieties for the future. Steven had been her sheet-anchor for so long, but soon she would have to face up to life on her own. In another month she would be well enough to go back to teaching – not now, perhaps, for the job required reserves of stamina she did not possess, but a post would be found for her whenever she was able to resume; the Education Department had assured her of that. Strange how large areas of her brain were functioning normally, yet the memory of personalities and places was denied to her. That would come! She clung to the belief as stubbornly as a convert, praying for it, with trembling fervour, almost mesmerizing herself that she had not lost that invaluable thing, her confidence, her self-assurance.

Luke, missing her at breakfast, had his work cut out to gain a few uninterrupted moments of her time. He carried a cup of coffee out on to the veranda and handed it to her in silence. She didn't look well this morning, her eyes faintly shadowed, a fine-drawn tension to her face, and he guessed at her sleepless night. She took it from him, smiling like an exhausted child, and he waited in silence until she had finished it, then took her hand, drawing her down into the garden, letting the glorious wash of sunlight spill over them in a radiant benediction.

"Spare me a moment, Andrea?" he asked gently.

She looked at him in surprise. "Why, of course, Dr. Freedman."

"Luke, please. It was Luke last night, remember?"

"Luke!" she smiled, seeing the concern in his eyes.

In truth he was rather dejected as he wondered how best to start the conversation, fearfully worried by Gillian's disclosures. Feeling the way he did about the child, he felt he just had to warn her. She seemed so delicately civilised in such a lushly tropical setting, yet Gillian Courtney was as tall and flamboyant as a canna lily. Pity young Andrea if she was even forced into competition with such a tigress. The thought was like a heavy swag on his shoulders.

Her clear eyes were measuring him, sensing his hesitation, guessing his plan.

"You're worried, aren't you, Luke?" She turned away to gaze long at the larkspur ranges, realising with a failing of the heart that her eyes were resting on a much loved sight. It would be lonely without love, without family, without friends, almost an outcast. "You're wondering if I've thought about the future?"

"Yes!" He knew by her tone she could read his mind and he felt a subtle warmth at the thought.

"I *have*!" she assured him with an expressionless little comment, turning to confront him. "Often! I can go back to my old job, you know!"

"Not yet, my dear!" he counselled, quietly emphatic. "The teaching profession is a strenuous one and quite frankly, I don't think you'll be up to it for quite some time yet!"

"What else can I do?" she asked simply. It was a gravely considered question and her clear grey eyes were hard to avoid.

The intensity of his feelings resounded through his

131

voice. "You must know, Andrea, you've always been a very special person to me, not just a case. I want to help you in every way I can. Would you let me think about something for you? Things crop up from time to time. A fill-in position, nothing too demanding, until you're strong enough to go on with your own work!"

Some hidden element of concern was echoing through his voice, focusing her attention.

"What's worrying you, especially, Luke? Something is!"

He looked at her a shade wryly. "You've a very delicate perception!"

"Is it Gillian?" she asked, cutting to the heart of the matter.

"What makes you say that?"

"No dark mystery!" She reached out a hand to a creamy pale frangipani blossom. "The air was electric between you last night. You don't like her, do you?"

"Not the least little bit!" he asserted with wry humour. "And the age of chivalry is indeed dead!" His blue eyes sobered abruptly. "It's you I'm concerned about, Andrea. I feel I should tell you that she's deeply attached to Daintree."

"I know that!" Her face appeared to pale, but he was unable to plumb the depths of her eyes, for she turned her profile to him. "Is that what you were talking about last night?"

"Not specifically!" He was forced into the half lie, fearing to admit the whole truth. "She just happened to mention in passing that she considered herself hot favourite in the marriage stakes!"

His attempt at the light touch didn't quite come off. She went even paler.

"I don't think Steven is thinking along those lines!"

she hazarded.

It could have been the truth or a monstrous error. He couldn't even rely on his own judgement – not with a man like Daintree. That was the sum of it. "Sometimes a determined woman can swing the balance," he suggested, shrugging his shoulders almost painfully.

"Can *you* see a woman getting the best of Steven?" she asked quietly.

"It would seem rather implausible!" he was forced to agree. "But she's ruthless and ambitious and she *has* got Helena Daintree on her side – no small thing, I'm sure you'll agree. I just wouldn't care to see you get caught in their crossfire!"

There was a melancholy line to the bend of her head. "Life moves on, doesn't it?" she said with a sound of regret. "We can't stand still for any length of time no matter what fate befalls us. We're only allowed a breathing space, then it's time to pick up the burden. I suppose that's all we're entitled to in the end!"

He moved his hand aimlessly, feeling utterly wretched. Her pallor, under the pale gold skin tints, was vaguely alarming. "I've upset you, haven't I? Believe me, that was never my intention. I've been up half the damned night debating whether to broach the subject or not."

She turned to him in quick distress, solely on his account. "No, Luke! You were right to say what you did. I know you've my best interests at heart."

He seemed reassured, his expression lightening. "At the end of the month the hospital committee are holding their first function – a picnic race day, ball type of thing. It's on Bynyara Downs, a big sheep property towards the Central Downs. The ball is held in one of the big wool sheds, but don't let that put you off. It's usually a very grand affair, well sprinkled with millionaires and their

133

pampered and polished womenfolk. If you'll allow me, I should have something worked out for you by then. You'll be that much stronger as well. What do you say, my dear?"

"Thank you, Luke," she said quietly, and turned to look at him, her eyes grave and unsmiling.

"You seem a little depressed!" he persisted, unable to leave the subject alone, not wanting to leave her like that.

"Perhaps a little! I had the most fearful dreams last night – wild and disorganising. I used to have them in the hospital. Fragments of this and that. Nothing that made much sense, just enough to unsettle me and put me on edge – a dangerous state of mind that leaves me feeling very vulnerable and undefended."

He frowned in concentration. "You have sleeping pills?"

"Yes!"

"Try to do without them if you can. But if you can't, they'll do you no harm on the occasional night when things start to pile up on you." His face clouded a little as he looked over her shoulder. "There's so much I want to say to you, Andrea, and so little time. Here's Daintree now, to run me down to the strip. Are you coming?"

She couldn't ignore that look in his eyes, half plea, half sense of loss.

"Yes, of course. And, Luke . . ."

"Yes?"

"Thank you!" She put out her hand and touched his shoulder. "I know I have a real friend in you!"

He lowered his head to her and it struck him that foolishly, romantically, that he was building up a dream that might never reach a satisfying conclusion, but her smile was to stay with him for many long days after.

It was only when he had said his good-byes down at the airstrip that Luke remembered the medallion. He swung back just as he reached the Cessna's wing tip.

"Oh, Andrea?"

She moved swiftly towards him, closing the gap. "Yes, Luke?"

"Your medallion, my dear. I almost forgot it. You had it in the hospital." He dived into the breast pocket of his jacket and retrieved a small medal which he held in the centre of his palm.

The sun beat down on it, flashing out a bright copper glint that struck at her eyes and hammered through her brain. She was on shifting ground, the unbounded landscape tilting, a dizziness in her head.

I know he's out of fashion, but I'd like you to take him along all the same. St. Christopher, patron saint of travellers.

The face was a smiling blur, but the voice was a girl's; soft and whimsical. Her fingers froze on the little medal, yet it was warm to the touch.

Obeying a totally uncontrollable instinct, Luke bent his head and brushed her smooth petalled cheek.

"Take care, Andrea!" he said fervently. Then he was gone, climbing into the Cessna, leaving her driven in on herself in a self-induced trance. The twin engines flared into life, but she stood there hardly hearing, fine-tuned to the shadow images that fluttered on her anxious brain.

Steven moved towards her with alacrity and grasped her arms almost roughly, drawing her back off the strip.

"Good God, child, you can't stand there, though the warmth of that farewell might well hold you spellbound. I hope you reciprocated and promised the last dance on Bynyara?"

She didn't answer him at all, but nestled back against him like a frightened little animal. He didn't understand it at all, but frowned, his hands hard on her shoulders, his dark face above her.

"Andrea?"

She was trying desperately to grasp at something that was sliding out of reach. Perhaps for ever! That will-o'-the-wisp voice. She concentrated on the sound of it, light and whimsical. She could hear it now echoing dully like a voice in a tunnel.

"For God's sake, *wave!* " Steven admonished her, his voice taunting. "Don't fall down on the job now. What a contrary little wretch you are, Andrea. Poor old Freedman nearly didn't take off. Andrea?" His hand came under her chin, tipping her head back. Her behaviour might have been odd, but her face was quite simply *tormented*. He locked her virtually a prisoner within his arms, and turned her to face him. "You've remembered something?"

"But it's gone! It's gone! It's gone! " There was an element of hysteria in her voice. She began to beat a small fist against his chest in an agony of bitter frustration, hot over-wrought tears spilling on to her face. "It was *there*, and it's gone! "

Her voice was vaguely unbearable with its pent-up pathos. He found he couldn't take it, his strange eyes glittering.

"Stop it now, little one. You can't tear yourself to pieces this way. Andrea! " He shook her hard and her head lolled like a flower on a slender stalk. "Stop now. God, I'm sorry, but you're giving way to hysteria! " He let his eyes fall on her small beaten face. "Listen to me, Andrea, it *will* come back! "

Her silence was chilling, a frightening thing.

"Don't you think I know how you feel?" he said harshly.

She shook her head, the effect of looking into his dark face just as she had known it would be. "You don't want me to remember, Steven. You told me!"

"I've changed my mind!" he said curtly. "I want you to remember everything. I want you to remember Godden. You were his fiancée. You must have loved him."

"I *didn't*! I *didn't*!" She hit him again in a frenzy, a rain of small blows to which he seemed oblivious.

He held her hard, cruelly intent, a line of concentration between his winged brows. "How do you *know*?"

"I didn't! I didn't," she repeated dully. "I've never loved anyone. But I hate you, Steven! You're so ... so ...!" She broke down, defeated, and collapsed against him, crying as if her heart would break, swamped by a feeling that soon she would lose him and in doing so, lose all trace of herself.

A dynamic inner intensity was etched on his face. "You'll remember!" he said tautly. "You've *got* to!" He caressed her small head and a faint wry smile softened his mouth. "If Freedman can still see us, he's in for a few bad nights! Come now, little one, I'm not going to allow you to upset yourself. You've been very brave up until now." The expression in his eyes might almost have been tenderness.

"Not *me*!" She lifted her head, her glance long and searching.

His hand was gently raking her curls, soothing away her mortal hurt. "Yes, *you*! The first time I saw you I saluted your courage."

"Did you, Steven?" All that mattered was a look in his eyes she wanted to cling to for ever, flooding her with a healing warmth.

"Yes!" he said briefly, his free hand brushing her throat. "I thought how beautiful you were and how desirable. But I'm not the first man to tell you that. Some time you're going to remember Carl Godden. And now is as good a time as any to tell you I've been withholding a few letters from his mother."

Very gently he was encasing her face between his hands. Her voice was a ghost whisper. "For *me*?" she asked, making the discovery that the tension was easing out of her. "Did you read them?"

"I haven't," he said carefully, "but it cost me an effort and they would, at a guess, have cost you a deal more. Perhaps tomorrow I'll let you have them. I can't withhold them indefinitely and you're showing a marked improvement in lots of ways. Come on now, dry your eyes, though you would seem to have done that on my shirt!"

"I'm sorry!" She pulled away a little, breathless.

"There's no need to be! When you're young and tormented and fancy yourself alone, you're entitled to a few tears!"

"You told me once you couldn't abide weeping women!"

He stretched out his hand and they walked back to the jeep. "But you're just a child," he said with the same old teasing glint. "A silky soft, sweetly smelling, baby girl-child, and quite the prettiest I've ever known!"

His voice was calm, casual even, and the terrible doubts and indecisions began to melt from her eyes.

The next few days passed uneventfully, but towards the end of the week, a party of American breeders and buyers flew in en route for the Channel Country and Steven's time was almost completely taken up with them. The three women, in reality anything but compatible, were forced back on their own company, a state of affairs that Gillian, in particular, seemed to find irksome. An accomplished rider, without being in the least a good horsewoman, for she had no real feeling for her mounts, she spent a great deal of her time riding the property, setting out on deliberately planned "accidental" jaunts to intercept Steven and the rest of the party.

Andrea, however, was content to take each day as it came. To her surprise and gratification she had discovered that Netta possessed considerable artistic ability, painting the most brilliant abstract designs that seemed entirely different from anything Andrea had ever seen – fantastic, imaginative, closely involved colours and patterns, full of movement and balance, essentially aboriginal, a break away from the traditional totemic art, yet they could not possibly have been mistaken for a white woman's art. She worked with an ordinary box of watercolours, an old tin full of brushes and a considerable stock of art paper sent out from her old Mission.

That morning the girls sat on a large green rug in the blossoming shade of the bauhinias a distance from the house, with Andrea holding up one stylistic pattern after another, previous efforts of Netta's, examining them carefully with a sympathetic and informed eye.

"That one not bad!" Netta broke off from her work to bestow the careless accolade.

"Not bad at all!" Andrea seconded laconically. "Have you ever tried your hand at landscapes, Netta?"

"You're jokin', miss." Netta showed her even, white teeth. "Not allowed. This kinda stuff all right. Women's work!" For a moment her highly polished, intelligent young face looked defiant and Andrea studied her thoughtfully. Netta, she knew, had been educated in a Methodist Mission, but the tribal traditions were as old

139

as time, inbred and slow to die out. A coloured woman would never dream of usurping the hereditary rights of the male, and consequently large areas of creative expression were denied to her by the tribal taboos imposed on her sex. Sent from the Mission to Mokhana at the age of fifteen, Netta in her first two weeks at the homestead had absorbed every painting in the house, their visual impact making a profound impression on her, inspiring her subsequent form of self-expression.

"I think there should be an outlet for your talent!" Andrea observed in a soft thoughtful voice. "It seems to me you're a born artist, but you're not developing your gifts."

Netta smothered a giggle, not overly impressed by her "gifts", but she cast a warm look of friendship over the white, satin-skinned girl who sat by her side. "I'll show you how to do them, seein' you like them so much. Nothin' to it, miss."

"Don't you believe it!" Andrea said firmly. "Here, let me show you. It's simple for you, Netta, but your artistic impulse is unique to your race."

Netta was silent, a little at a loss, like a black butterfly watching Andrea take out a fresh brush and a clean piece of paper beginning her own composition, deliberately trying to imitate the coloured girl's style. She had a certain facility of her own that became quickly apparent, but the pattern, when it was finished, basically the same in design and executed with perfect correctness, simply did not measure up to Netta's in movement or dramatic impulse. The original was unquestionably the superior work of art.

"Nothin' wrong with *that*!" Netta said in a kind, encouraging voice, privately itching to add just a little "this and that" to give the pattern more freedom.

Andrea smiled at her dead give-away expression before Netta turned back to her own design. It seemed to Andrea's eye to evolve without preliminary sketches or even forethought, but miraculously it turned out just right in the end. Both girls, thoroughly preoccupied, were startled when Gillian broke through the trees, cantering Rimfire the big bay gelding towards them. She slowed to a walk and came in alongside them.

Netta looked up with a quick, shy smile, but Gillian ignored her in such a way as to suggest she was invisible to the naked eye, addressing herself, drawlingly, to Andrea.

"Kindergarten out in the fresh air. How charming!" She slanted a disparaging glance over Andrea's silvery fair head. "You don't ride, do you? It seems very odd, to say the least, on a cattle station!" Inexplicably she moved the mare in very close to them and Netta sprang to her feet instinctively, one hand protectively on Andrea's shoulder, feeling the deep tremble that ran through the white girl's body. Andrea was still sitting, apparently jolted by shock, her eyes on the satiny flanks of the gelding.

"What an absolute ninny!" Gillian observed unpleasantly. "Don't tell me you're frightened? The best cure for timidity is to get out and try your hand at it. If there was any urgency at all about it I'd give you a few lessons myself, but you won't be staying on that much longer, will you, so Helena was saying." She shrugged a shoulder and smiled briefly. "Well, I'm off! I'll leave you . . ." she glanced down almost contemptuously at the work sheets . . . "to your scribble patterns!"

"And good riddance, you bitch!" Netta murmured after her retreating back, her soft liquid vowels robbing the words of a great deal of their impact.

"Netta!" Andrea remonstrated halfheartedly.

"An' I jus' hope she fall off, but I don't suppose she will!" Netta continued obsessively. "Bitch! that's her real name all right, miss. Come to that, I could teach you myself. Ain't nothin' to ridin' once you know how!"

"I can ride, Netta," Andrea said gently.

Netta's glossy black head spun round, her curls dancing. There was no mistaking her surprise. "You sure, Miss Andrea? You never done any of it here."

"I know. But intuitively I feel I can ride. I couldn't be mistaken about a thing like that, could I?"

"I'm sure I don't know, miss," Netta repeated a little helplessly, floored by the "intuitively". She didn't look in the least impressed but downright anxious. Andrea, watching her expressive face, had to smile. "Come finish your scribble patterns," she said impishly, seeing that Netta took no offence whatsoever at the term. "Tonight I'm going to show them to Mr. Steven."

"Oh no, miss!" Netta flopped down on the rug again, disposing her wry young limbs. "You're out of your mind!"

"I'm not!" Andrea suddenly felt like laughing but remained poker-faced all the same. "You don't mind, do you?"

Netta gave her a naïvely fascinated look with a twin gleam of wistfulness and mischievousness.

"Well, I expect if you ain't got nothin' more serious to discuss!"

Andrea smiled and dipped her head, her own plan of action for the day quite clear. But to make things easier for Netta, her appointed guardian, she would have her try-out alone.

She gave herself no time to reconsider, but found her

way down to the stables in the early part of the afternoon, first making sure no one was about. Her mouth was dry with excitement and a certain apprehension. A woman's intuition was not always an infallible thing, but she was as certain as she was of anything that she *could* ride. Only her long convalescence had kept her interest in physical pursuits to a minimum. Only Jimmy, the slip of an aboriginal lad and a sure hand with horses, was about. She looked into the cool interior of the stables, dim now after the glare of the sun, saddles and gear merging into a shadowed blur.

Jimmy came out to meet her, beaming brightly. "Afternoon, miss. Everyone's away by now!"

Andrea smiled wryly. "I know. I want to go riding myself, Jimmy. Could you find me a mount?"

Jimmy's smiling vivacity was swept away like magic. His face betrayed polite incredulity, a deep unwillingness to offend and an overriding consternation. His velvety black eyes went blank. "I got a nice little mare, miss, gentle and ladylike – a good walker if you want a try-out!" He moved back to pat the russet neck of a slender little mare with soft, starry eyes.

The colt in the stall a few feet away was another matter. It tossed its small splendid head, its white blaze startling against the black satin of its coat, its hooves beating a restless tattoo on the ground.

"No use lookin' at that one, miss!" Jimmy counselled, shocked by the direction of her fixed stare, that unmistakable leap of love and admiration. She scarcely seemed to hear him, as her eyes slid over the colt's small, dynamic head, the long arched neck, the sliding, shining muscle power. Something inside of herself tightened, then uncoiled miraculously. She could see herself, her head low along the colt's gleaming neck, its silver plume flying, rac-

143

ing against the wind. She could feel the warm hide against her legs, the thrill of galloping over the grassy savannahs. Jimmy was surveying her with comical apprehension, aghast at those wide, eager eyes between their thick dark lashes. He had seen that special look before. The colt was perfection – bred of the warm starry skies and the grasslands, fiery with good blood and good living, plenty of temperament and a turn of speed like the west wind. He was no villain, but he was a spirited animal that needed mastery and a good pair of hands. This girl was no bigger than Netta, who looked down her nose at him, but Netta could ride anything.

The girl clucked to the colt and walked towards the stall, holding out her palm and breathing hard down her nostrils. Jimmy suddenly relaxed. She seemed to know what she was about and that heavy, warm breathing was a trick of his own. The colt pricked its ears with interest, then instantly responded, dropping its muzzle into the girl's hand, huffing in a kind of ecstasy.

"Saddle him up, Jimmy!" she said quietly, driven by a compulsion to take the colt over rising ground. She stood there for a moment dazzled by its spectacular beauty.

"He's Mr. Steve's!" Jimmy pointed out with gentle insinuation, making one last stand. "And that means he has plenty of spirit. You might find him hard to handle!"

"That's all right, Jimmy," Andrea said with half-feigned confidence. "I'll take full responsibility!"

"You'll have to, miss. If anything happens to either of you, the Boss will skin me alive!"

Andrea smiled. "I'm willing to gamble that I'm equal to the colt. Besides, he knows me, don't you, my beauty, my lovely one?" She fell to caressing the colt's glossy neck, her mind full of its superb lines.

Jimmy gave way with admirable grace. They stood on

either side of the colt, giving it loving attention, until the little mare a few feet away whinnied pathetically, hating to be ignored.

"Another time, sweetheart!" Andrea promised, looking over at those starry, imploring eyes. Jimmy grinned and darted away smartly to select a saddle for the colt. He walked the beautiful animal out to the saddling rail, showing off its lovely swaying walk under the blazing sunlight. The colt took the girthing up perfectly, then Andrea swung its head away from the rail and prepared to mount. Jimmy gave her a leg-up and she was up in the saddle with sure, instinctive grace, knowing a burst of elation that nearly swamped her with its intensity. How could she have forgotten the joy of being in the saddle? She touched the reins lightly and the colt moved off with only a mild, excited reefing.

"Don't worry, Jimmy," she called over her shoulder, "I know what I'm about!"

He could see the excitement blazing out of her eyes and he swung up a hand in acknowledgment, liking the set of her shoulders, the easy fluid style. She knew how to ride all right. What a puzzle!

"Don't go too far out, miss," he called after her. "Take it easy this first time out!"

His words echoed faintly, lost among multiple new sensations. Five minutes later she was flying across the open grasslands, her slight, supple figure swaying effortlessly in the saddle. The colt was behaving beautifully, covering the ground with its long springy stride, seemingly as entranced as its youthful rider.

Andrea took deep breaths, filling her lungs with clean, aromatic air. The sun wind skittered cheerfully through the trees, sending showering blossom on to the wide brim of her hat. The whole world came alive in all its dimensions, wonderfully fresh and translucent. Budgerigars took to the infinite blue skies in one flight, with a colour wave of emerald and flashes of yellow and down on the river flats, stock were grazing, their heads bent mutely to the lush herbage, some fording the narrow rock strewn crossing to the other side. An arc of fire burned along the horizon so that the ranges spiralled like burnished temples to the Sun God. It was a clear, colour-washed world, the rich red of the earth, the multiple greens of the trees and the grasses, the silver glitter of the long, lovely chain of billabongs.

Tiny white and gold daisies swam like fish on the crest of the bent grasses, swishing against the colt's sleek sides. It seemed to Andrea that the savannah was a mosaic of colour with broad pockets of shadows under the trees, caverns of pure green. The wind softly ruffled the colt's silver plume and she lowered her face along its gleaming neck and gave it its head.

The sunlight was slanting now, falling obliquely, and an eagle soared and sailed far away above them in the vivid blue. Andrea, unknowing, was undergoing a gradual transformation, an intoxication almost, things felt in the blood and never seen. The remote recesses of her mind began stirring up visions, only now she did nothing to frustrate them with frantic bursts of concentration, or in a sense, repression, but let them come in long unbroken waves of established rhythm.

"Now watch this, Andy, it's not too difficult!"

The vision was accurate to the last detail, as clear as a bell. A man and a small girl with white gold plaits standing in a grassy paddock, a compact little grey pony between them, the child's face turned up to the man with implicit love and trust. It was her father. The pony was

146

Mimi, of course, the great joy of the childhood.

"*Leave the reins light now in Mimi's mouth!*" The child's eyes were earnestly screwed up against the strong sunlight.

Another vision flared in front of her eyes. A small girl crushed up against her father's tweed jacket; both looking out over the limitless iridescent ocean.

"When we get to Australia, I'm going to buy you a pony. Would you like that?"

"Will it really be mine?" The soft voice was full of a child's wonder.

The manner of her awakening was beyond her control. With a half fearful joy she realised she was crossing distance and time. Her mouth felt dry and her cheeks burning hot. She reined the colt in under the feathery acacias that lined the banks of the lily lagoon, her memories coming stronger, obtrusive now, creating in her the urgency for perfect quietness of body. She fell face down in the long grass, hearing the measured thud of her heart, the agony of self-questionings over.

The colt looked across at her, silent and profoundly serious as though conscious of the solemnity of the moment, then it fell, contentedly, to cropping over the grass within easy circumference. For a long time she lay there, her head a kaleidoscopic whirl of incidents, no further refinements of an old torment, but the halcyon days of her childhood; the fine careless days she had thought forever wiped clean from her memory.

The past shifted and played across her small face. They had lived on a small farm in the beautiful Goulburn Valley of Victoria. It had taken all her father's savings, but almost immediately it had begun to show a quick return. They had been very happy, the three of them; her mother, her father, herself and the menagerie of pets she

147

always surrounded herself with. She had barely started high school when her mother had gone into hospital for major surgery and slipped out of life in the post-operative stages. The blow had been crippling at a time when they had cherished the hope that she had safely come through the worst.

Her father had never really recovered. He had sold up the farm at once, finding the small, comfortable farmhouse they had all once loved unbearable. They had come up to Queensland, clinging closer than ever now, though this marked the period when her father's health began its slow decline.

Most of the money had gone on her expensive education, but she had repaid her father's sacrifices by graduating with first-class honours. He had been so proud of her.

My golden girl! My Andrea! If only your mother could be with us now!

It was her mother's name he had died with on his lips less than a year later. Andrea turned her face into her hands in a storm of emotion, crying, not bitterly, but for the unrecoverable, the pain of loss and deepest nostalgia. Then suddenly it was over, her pent-up emotions subsided. She pushed up and walked down the sandy banks to the billabong, and bent to the stream, cupping her hands and filling them with water, splashing her face repeatedly. Calm and a sense of purpose came to her. She would have to write again to Irina Godden, but first she would have to find . . . *Liane*.

CHAPTER VIII

It was late when Andrea rode into the home paddock and it took her a few seconds to realise that she was being watched. Jimmy, she thought, with a quirk of amusement, anxious to save both their necks. She brought the colt in briskly and slid off his back, patting him lovingly, calling over her shoulder:

"I'm back, Jimmy! All in one piece!"

"Well, that's *something*, at least!"

The voice, terse and resonant with a fine goading edge, could only have been Steven's. She whirled with an involuntary shiver, starting to say something that suddenly died on her. Her eyes ranged anxiously over his face. It was apparent, at once, that his emotions were not under their usual impeccable control, for he looked, quite simply, a man to be feared. A stranger – dangerous, tall and very formidable, his eyes an aquamarine blaze in his dark face, a muscle jerking beside his mouth.

She felt the first faint tremor run through her.

"*Not* Jimmy!" he said very gently, and she could feel his tension. "Only big brother Steve, doing his usual watchdog act because every time I turn my back something quite lunatic happens. Do you realise I've been nearly out of my mind wondering if you'd taken a toss or worse?"

The sunlight shafted across her bare head, gleaming like a silvery cap; her hat hung by its strap down her back. Her face was glowing, impregnated with colour whipped up under the skin, her eyes enormous. There was something different about her, he saw, some lack of restraint,

149

like spring water effervescing from sandstone into the sunlight, pure and tingling. Whatever it was, it fanned his anger.

She swallowed and her throat rippled. "I'm sorry, Steven!" she made a little placating gesture with her hand which he ignored and she threw up her head, showing the smooth cream of her throat, almost inviting him to touch her there, he thought grimly. "Were you anxious?"

When confronted with her quiet serenity it pushed him right over the edge.

"You're *sorry!*" he exploded, injecting a breathtaking dynamism into the word. "It strikes me that that's a totally inadequate word! You might consider I didn't even know you *could* ride, let alone handle the colt!" With a controlled sort of desperation he turned away to quieten the animal, unbuckled the saddle and threw it over the fence, then turned the colt off into the succulent, rain-fed grasses. He looked alert and hard, all flowing muscles, totally male. She could hardly take her eyes off him with a build-up of suspense. She saw the jewelled flash of his eyes. "I've torn a few strips off Jimmy, let me tell you," he bit off.

"But that's dreadful!" A tiny blue vein pulsated in her throat, a give-away.

It appeared to give him some satisfaction, for his eyes fell on it. "Yes, isn't it?" he agreed. "And that's the last time you're going to do anything like that!" He moved across to her with his soundless, cat-like tread and if she tried to retreat he didn't seem to notice it. "I've selected you as the only woman I know who could drive me insane!"

She managed a husky little laugh, unnerved by his tone, holding her fist in a tight little grip against her racing heart. "I said I'm sorry, Steven. Do you want me to go down on my knees and apologise? I'd no idea you'd get so het up. I haven't harmed the colt in any way. In fact, we went beautifully. Friends right from the start!"

He drew a sharp, hostile breath, his white teeth snapping.

"*Friends!* How sweet!" his eyes roved over her as if he found her unbelievable. "I suppose a girl like you is bound to have one or two drawbacks. Right at this moment there's nothing I'd like better than to give you a good slap, but failing that . . ."

She stared back at him, rooted to the spot, almost bemused. He was pale under that teak tan, the lines from nostril to mouth more deeply pronounced. One hand reached out for her, closed in at her narrow waist, sliding up the small of her back; the other caught her under the chin, turning her mouth up.

Excitement spurted through her, disturbingly sudden, the touch of him stirring a pain like a fever. He kissed her with a dangerous, stinging sweetness, that still had the power to dispel tension between them, so that her mouth parted of its own accord. She had no thought of denying him this form of punishment if that was what was intended. But it didn't turn out that way. Instinctively she shut her eyes and lifted her hand to lie along his lean, hard cheek, her fingertips sensitized to the tantalising smooth rasp.

His sharp intake of breath came against her own mouth and she felt her own breath shorten, her heart fluttering as with a shot of adrenalin. He drew back into the shadow of the doorway, his hands slipping along the curve of her back, more confident than any she could have imagined. Dappled greeny-gold highlights fell queerly across his high cheekbones.

"Ten minutes ago I was spitting mad. I don't know

what I'd have done to you then, now I only want to make love to you. Funny, isn't it?" His eyes roamed over each separate feature of her face, her mouth softly pulsing, framed for kissing. He moved abruptly, and sunlight speared across his eyes in a searing glare. "I've wanted you since I first laid eyes on you – but you know that!"

She moistened her mouth with the tip of her tongue. "No!"

"*Yes!*" he said tautly. "You know it. Why bother to deny it?"

Colour rushed up under her skin. She looked so fresh and so wild and so beautiful that he caught her to him with a half-blind frustration, kissing her with a passion and an urgency, a dark frightening energy, that undermined every scrap of her resistance. It swept her down a long corridor towards brilliant light, an intense illumination that threatened to overcome her. It made her afraid. She wasn't herself any more, only what Steven wanted of her. She twisted away, wrenching her head aside. She needed time, time to sort out her own mind, time to dispel all the shadows that hung about her. Her head was tilted back against his arm. She stared up at him with an odd pleading, the pupils of her eyes dilating.

"Why?" he said harshly.

"Wanting is not loving, Steven!" she said in a voice so brittle it might shatter like glass.

"Did I say that it was?"

"No, you didn't!" Her face that had been so disturbingly beautiful and uninhibited was now closing like a flower.

There was a hint of self-contempt in his voice.

"Would you have believed me if I said that I loved you?"

"No!"

"So what's the difference?" he asked with deep cynicism. His eyes had lost that look of stormy vitality. They went cold. He wore a look of glittery arrogance she couldn't fail to recognise, chilling as winter steel.

"An infinite difference to *me*!" she pointed out carefully, looking away from his dark face as though she found the sight of it unbearable. A curious feeling of pathos was sweeping over her, making her eyes shimmer like fresh water lakes. Finally he spoke.

"Who was it who said, true love is in short enough supply. Seize it where you find it with both hands!" His voice turned wry, even laconic. "What would *they know*?" He relaxed his grasp abruptly and looked down at her still creamy face. "How serious we're becoming! If it means anything to you at all, little one, I've never told a woman I wanted her in my life! You've *that* distinction, however unwelcome!" He looked down at her with cold, interested eyes. "You might consider before you start out on your next unauthorised little jaunt, to let me know. That way, you won't invite trouble!"

"I'll consider it very carefully," she said suddenly, and he saw on her face a look he had never seen before – a delicate determination, a spirited little air of self-assurance. He would remember it vividly. His eyes narrowed to slits and his voice underwent a rapid change, sharpening with renewed interest.

"So what else is new, little sphinx?" He made one of his lightning moves and caught the point of her shoulder to spin her towards him.

"You know me rather well, don't you?" she said silkily.

"Not nearly well enough!"

Andrea felt faintly giddy. His voice had moved back to the sphere of the senses and he felt her shoulder lose its resistance and curve to the palm of his hand. It was the moment to confide in him. Neither of them, as intensely preoccupied as duellists, saw Gillian's approach. She jerked to a halt at the sight of them, the muscles of her throat rigid and strained so that her voice came as a hoarse whisper, shrivelled with hate.

"Off with the old and on with the new! The natural order of things, I suppose?"

Steven turned on her with slick urbanity. "Come along in, Gill. Don't stand outside missing anything!"

She stalked towards them, elemental, feline, outraged.

"You fool, Steve, can't you see how things are going with this girl? All that helpless femininity! It makes me *sick*! She's madly dependent on you and all you do is encourage it!"

"Obviously it hasn't struck you that kind of woman might appeal to me," he said with a smooth gentleness that might have given her pause.

"Not *you*!" She jerked up her head in denial, her scarlet mouth working. "You want a woman as self-reliant as yourself!"

"You think so?" His head was thrown back a little, his eyes half closed, as arrogant as the devil.

"You realise people are beginning to talk?" She let loose that statement on the fine edge of frenzy, the sight of Andrea standing almost hypnotised under Steven's hand obliterating her senses.

Steven's face hardened to granite. "My dear Gill!" he said with weary sarcasm. "That's of little consequence to me. People have been 'talking' since they first gathered in caves. But in this particular instance every last, lurid imagining could so easily be squelched!"

Gillian's face crumpled abruptly, abandoning to an abyss of panic she herself had precipitated. "You can't

154

do this to me, Steven!"

"Now that's a clever trick of the trade!" he said admiringly.

Under his hand Andrea tensed like a sapling to resist the storm, her profile softening to compassion. She could never like Gillian, but she could feel her pain. "There's no need to put yourself through this torment, Miss Courtney," she said slowly, each word a blade that could plunge to the heart. "I'm quite willing to free Steven of my suffocating clutches. I'm going back where I belong – or more accurately where I lived and worked. And very soon!"

Without a word Steven locked her two wrists in one single grip. "Don't be absurd!"

His voice was so harshly emphatic that it gave her a fleeting, ebbing warmth.

"But she's right, don't you see?" Reddish lights glowed in Gillian's eyes. "She can't stay here indefinitely – Luke Freedman said as much, and he'd be only too pleased to help her along. Besides, you must know Helena doesn't want her here!"

"Does Helena want any woman here?" he asked with such bitter irony that Gillian stared at him, shocked. He gave her a look that was wholly arrogant. "All three of you might remember that Mokhana belongs to me. I make the decisions big and small because that's the way I am. Take it or leave it!"

"Well, I for one will leave it!" Andrea said in a fierce little voice, and tried to break free, stung by his tone. "Please, Steven, let me go. I'll leave you and Miss Courtney to it!"

He reduced all her struggles to impotence, locking her hands against his side. His voice was flat, even bored.

"That's very considerate of you, little one, but quite

unnecessary! I'm sure Gillian has something better to do with her time. God knows I'm not fool enough to fall in with the plan!"

Gillian made a sound of strangled distress, then whirled on her heel and stumbled back to the house to unleash her story on Helena's willing ears.

"How cruel you are, Steven!" Andrea said, unnaturally quiet. Each word fell like a stone from her lips.

"Cruel?" There was a world of mockery in the one syllable. "I'm *that*, because you won't let me be anything else!" His strange eyes were lit with a power of concentration. "Tell me, pretty faun, what did you expect of me? An act of dementia? Marry Gillian to stop her from talking? That calls for a brand of courage I haven't got. I saw Gillian sit through her father's funeral, if not exactly smiling, then perfectly dry-eyed, for the simple reason that he left her and her gadfly mother a cool quarter of a million dollars to fritter away on world trips and Italian counts and wardrobes of dresses. What worthier causes?"

"But you made love to her, encouraged her!"

"I'm as full of faults as the next man!" he said with crisp insolence. "I've made love to a lot of women, but none of them have held a gun on me to marry them!" His voice took on a hard, challenging directness. "I feel no shame for my peccadilloes – does that shock you, my innocent? I'm not, after all, a country parson. In my position, women are a perfectly permissible eccentricity!"

She could feel the heat under her skin, his taunting eyes on her face. From somewhere she found her own bitter-sweet voice:

"And that's what I am? . . . a perfectly permissible eccentricity to be hoarded up?" She flung her shimmering glance challengingly into his dark face.

A wild kind of anger prowled in his eyes. "I haven't inexhaustible patience, little one, so have a care! If you were what you're trying to make out, would I bother hoarding you up, as you put it?"

He saw her face tauten under pressure, giving fair warning. Her hand flew up of its own accord in a swift flare of anger. It was suddenly hard to remember she loved him. She hated him. *Hated* him! It was a little while before she could see him again clearly, for he had her under control, locked up tight against him, his voice near her head hard and authoritative.

"Will you stop all this unbridled nonsense, before I really hurt you. Whatever you think, it's prejudiced by emotion. I didn't precipitate this row, *you* did. *You* and Gill with her warped insinuations. You told me once that you owed me your life. You owe me nothing, but I demand the right to know what's best for you. I never at any time regarded Gillian Courtney as any more than bright company. I've made love to her, but we've never been lovers – is that what you want to know? She sought *me* out, if I may be so ungallant. I made her no promises, said nothing that she could possibly misconstrue. She has a natural predilection for hankering after the impossible, you know!"

There was a kind of bewilderment in her voice.

"You don't have to explain yourself to me, Steven!"

"No, damn it, I *don't*!" he said with soft irony.

She shook her head fretfully from side to side. "I want to go back to the place where I lived before my accident. There are things about myself I must find out!" Somehow she found the strength to look up into his face. His eyes were brilliant, narrowed intently upon her. If she didn't look away from him now she would drown, she thought, as she fought the craving to go into his arms.

"I want to go by myself!" she said hardily.

"Well, you damned well *won't*! Discard that one as a phantom hope! Do you think I want that kind of thing on my mind? I've got work to do. I can't be wondering what you're getting up to day in and day out!"

"Do you *have* to wonder?" For a few seconds she was caught in the quicksand of hope.

"I think so! At this stage, at any rate. Don't overestimate your strength, little one. One short tussle and your heart races under my hand!"

Long fingers of shadow stole across the ground. "I can't fight you, Steven," she said with soft desolation. "You're someone I can't withstand however hard I try. I just want to go back. You must understand!"

He kept silent for a moment, looking down at her shining pale head.

"All right, all right!" he said gently, tracing a finger along the curve of her cheek with that curious power to release her tensions. "I said I'll take you and I will. While we're there, you might buy something cripplingly expensive to dazzle Freedman at the ball. I wouldn't worry about whether he discussed you with Gillian or not. Gillian can turn the minutest grain of truth to her advantage. Freedman is not without integrity, but he's not the man for you, little one. Sad, but true!"

Dinner was ghastly, like taking a stroll through a minefield, expecting at each step to have the scene blow up in one's face. But it was got through. *Got through* were the only words Andrea could think of to describe the state of cold war that existed, concealed by a deadly cloak of cold civility with promises of the skirmishes, the hit and run raids, the secretive feline manoeuvres, to come.

Andrea was a little surprised at her own poise, not real-

158

ising that this was a good omen, for each day she grew stronger and stronger. After many long weeks of living in a vacuum she was picking up the threads of her old life. Morning dawned so bright and beautiful it didn't seem possible anything bad could happen. The freight delivery plane flew in on schedule and Gillian was ready, having not the slightest difficulty in arranging a lift to the Coast. She stalked out of the house wrapped in cold fury, with only the saving grace of a word to her hostess, enlisting the aid of a station hand to drive her down to the strip.

With Steven busy, apparently oblivious to the cross-currents, giving the men instructions for the day, Helena lost no time in gaining a face-to-face confrontation. She followed Andrea out to the veranda, where Netta, fussing over her as usual, had set up Andrea's mid-morning cup of coffee. Her face was quite unreadable, but Andrea knew what was coming.

"Don't run away, my dear," Helena said very softly, a danger signal. "I want to talk to you."

"I wasn't running, Miss Daintree," Andrea retorted composedly. "I was merely stiffening my spine!"

"Not so wishy-washy, are we?"

Andrea put her own interpretation on that. "I am feeling stronger, yes!"

Helena sat down on a white wrought iron chair and adjusted it carefully. "Good! I'm very pleased to hear it, for now we can get down to hard facts!" She inclined her head regally. "Gillian is my godchild. I'm very fond of her. If and when Steven marries I would prefer it to be a young woman of whom I know and approve – Gillian, to be precise."

Andrea's eyes came back from a long trip around the garden. "Tell me one thing, does Steven have any say in this?"

Helena gave her a cold look. "Don't be smart, my dear! Steven is, as his father was, a law unto himself. But I like to think I have some special influence!"

"But is it that simple, Miss Daintree? What if Steven has no such plan?"

Helena's dark gaze swept her from head to foot. "Would you know, my dear?"

"I think so!" Andrea retorted unexpectedly.

For a moment Helena looked almost comically stunned, then she recovered. "Stretching the point to the unseemly and the ridiculous, a girl like you I could *never* tolerate. You have a nagging resemblance to Vivienne, not in looks but in style. The soft touch, it never fails . . . *for a while!* Vivienne was the same."

Even with her head turned away Andrea was conscious of those coal-black eyes. "Don't undersell me, Miss Daintree. I'm not Vivienne and neither, I think, does Steven share your nature as perhaps his father did. Steven still loves his mother to this day, though he'd rather die than admit it!"

Helena gave a laugh that was like the tinkle of ice cubes. "Does he try to contact her in any way? Of course he doesn't, my dear!"

Andrea couldn't deny it. "With Steven the woman would always have to bend first," she said, conscious there was latent pain in each word. "His mother bitterly rejected him. He's never forgiven it!"

"But she didn't reject him, my dear." Helena smiled for the first time as if she saw a pleasant picture in her head. "It was quite pathetic really and I would have helped her if I could, but my path was clear cut. Garth would never have surrendered his son and he had a great deal of power and money. Vivienne had nothing! Even a perverse kind of pride kept her from accepting a more

160

than generous settlement. All the letters, of course, I destroyed. I always endeavour to follow the logical dictates. It was either Garth or Vivienne, and naturally my loyalty was to my brother. Steven would have been adversely affected by their constant wrangling – although, to be strictly fair, Vivienne never did make a scene of any kind. Had Steven gone with his mother he would have gained nothing. As it is he has Mokhana, a great inheritance." She was speaking slowly, painstakingly as though she was explaining the situation to a rather dense child.

There was a note of abhorrence in Andrea's soft voice. "And you never told him his mother wrote to him?"

Helena shook her dark head. "My dear girl! Where's your intelligence? Why would I? What good would it have done? It would only have unsettled him. He took it hard enough as it was. A few years of no response and Vivienne gave up. I'm only surprised she lasted as long as she did." She glanced at Andrea's bent head and gave a laugh of genuine amusement. "She married again, you know, some years back, and she has talent of a kind to keep her busy. I'm not entirely heartless, you know. The problem was that she was unsuited to Garth, to Mokhana. To all of us. As *you* are!"

Andrea ignored the last charge, too preoccupied with the first. Her grey eyes were extraordinarily clear and direct.

"What a burden you must have carried all these years, knowing you acted with such treachery!"

For the first time Helena showed a chink in her armour. An ugly flush rose to her throat. "My dear girl, you're incredible!" she gasped. "Vivienne might have said something like that. I felt no such thing. My loyalty is and always has been to my own kind, and believe me, Gillian is not beaten. I'm on her side, and you have yet to feel

161

the weight of my influence!"

"Forgive me if I'm not impressed!" Andrea's voice was not so much sarcastic as studiously grave.

Helena made a sound like an insidious hiss. "You *will* be, my dear. No one has ever offended me as you have, and you'll pay!" She didn't sound in the least dramatic, but icily sincere, her black eyes darting over Andrea's face. "You've come through one disaster. Careful this new one doesn't topple around your head!"

Andrea was conscious of a creeping chill for all the brilliant sunshine. "I could go to Steven with the facts. It's still not too late for him to do something about his mother. How she must have suffered, but one could wish she might have shown a little more spirit!" She turned her head sharply from the flash in Helena's eyes. "I don't know the true facts, but I can well imagine. I'll speak to Steven!"

Helena's face was one of dark confidence. "He very likely will think you unbalanced enough to say anything. He might even consider you need a psychiatrist as he's hinted in the past. You're not quite right, are you, my dear?"

Andrea considered this with wry humour. "I expect to start gibbering at any minute!"

"Ah yes!" Helena emitted a contemptuous sigh. "Just remember I've had Steven since he was a little boy. He'd never betray me!" Her cold dry tones were suddenly unbearable to Andrea's ears.

"The miracle is, he's never shaken you off!" she said, her voice changing, anger breaking over it.

"But he hasn't!" Helena's assurance was chilling. "Mokhana has always been my home. Vivienne made the mistake of thinking she could usurp me, poor unhappy creature. You, to my surprise, are not quite so ... *un-*

realistic, so listen here! The facts are simple. Mokhana and I belong together. Steven is my nephew, my beloved Garth's son. As for any other, I decided long ago that as Steven must marry to preserve our family and our heritage, Gillian must be the one, until her usefulness is ended or she behaves according to my plans!' "

It took a few seconds for Andrea to regain her breath. "It seems to me you're courting madness!" The words seemed wrenched from her.

Helena smiled thinly. "No one is saner than I am, my dear. I've always known what I wanted and how to get it. My sex has set its own limitation. It would have been so much better to have been born a man. My own dear father only wanted sons, splendid and fearless like Garth was. I always looked up to him, idolised him. I never met a man in my life to measure up to my father and brother. I faced up to the inevitable and never married. You might do the same!" She gave a laugh of cynical humour. "Not never *marry*, my dear, of course I can see you're one of those women who *must* lean on a man, but you might face this inevitability of leaving Mokhana. There's nothing for you here. I promise you you'll be much better off!" Her black eyes swept Andrea's face. "I can see this has hit you cruelly. You've lost all your colour. I prayed this situation would never arise, but it has. I didn't intend to be so brutal, but you left me no other course. Now I'm going to read a book and blot out all this unpleasantness. Steven is, I understand, taking you back where you belong. I imagine he is as relieved as I am. Men do tend to get bored with good works!" She stood up, flicking away an imaginary crease in her skirt. "If you're a smart girl, you'll disappear, just like that!"

Andrea looked up at her and her voice was soft and reasoned. "If the alternative was living with you, Miss

163

Daintree, I might just accept that!"

"That's quite enough!" Helena almost spat like a furious cat. "Insolence will do you no good. When you play for high stakes, my dear, you must be prepared to lose. Don't think I've automatically discounted what you did to Gillian. I have never seen the poor girl so shocked and distressed, but she had the good sense to enlist my aid!"

Andrea could feel her revulsion showing in her face, her stomach rebelling at the whole, ugly scene, but something drove her on, though Helena left her little space to manoeuvre. "I think 'the poor girl' will only enlist your aid as long as it suits her!" she hazarded, her voice very dry and urbane. "She has a nice flair for ruthlessness herself!"

Helena was equal to it, shaking her silver-winged dark head. "Then she will find to her sorrow that she's overreached herself – as *you* have! Now why don't you ring for more coffee? I see that has gone cold." She glanced negligently over her shoulder. "May I take it you're leaving?"

"Believe me, Miss Daintree, my sole interest at the moment is to do just that!"

"Then the whole issue is simplified!" Helena said pleasantly. "On second thoughts, don't get up, my dear. I'll get Netta to bring out fresh coffee. We must look to your personal well-being, mustn't we?"

"Why not, as this is a Jekyll and Hyde situation?" Andrea retorted very smartly indeed.

"No, dear!" Helena continued just as pleasantly. "You simply wouldn't suit at all. But sit back and enjoy the sun while you can. I suppose it's the last time in your life you'll be exposed to such affluence!"

"Perhaps!" Andrea said lightly, "but I don't regret for one moment having had such a profound human experience. If I'd have read about you, I would never have believed it! Thank you, again. With a friend like you it's proved utterly unnecessary to have an enemy, and you've provided me with a fascinating insight into the behavioural pattern of animal of another species, the possessive woman!"

Helena reeled, driven by some dark uncontrollable force. She moved so suddenly that the table rocked, then she reached for the small silver coffee pot and hurled it with hate and ferocity. "You insufferable little bitch!"

It should have slammed right into Andrea, but she simply wasn't there. She flung herself clear, alerted with instant perception to the woman's underlying viciousness.

She shrugged off her shock and her white face. "You've put a dint in that, haven't you? Charming and probably irreplaceable. You're slipping, Miss Daintree!" She straightened up and adjusted the table. "I can't apologise for anything," she said sombrely. "You had that coming. Let's say I regard it as a strike for Vivienne. Now why don't you collect your heirloom silver, because I'm going!"

With her silver-gilt head up she walked past Helena's tall, menacing figure, while Helena continued to look out over the garden in the most peculiar fashion, her dark face almost gaunt.

CHAPTER IX

ANDREA got a taxi just as it discharged its fare outside one of the big department stores. She asked the driver to take her to her hotel. It was no distance, she could have walked, but he nodded laconically with no sense of reproach. That was how he picked up a lot of his fares; dispirited ladies who couldn't manage that last hundred yards. Andrea sat back, trying to relax, if only briefly. She felt almost lightheaded with exhaustion and she hadn't had a bite to eat since breakfast.

The city looked deeply familiar, amiably thrusting, under cloudless skies with an engaging sub-tropical air, a faintly indolent charm peculiar to the warmer climates. The weather was beautiful, the crisp blue and golden days of autumn into winter, and a new fountain was playing. She closed her eyes briefly. Her mind seemed to be spinning around in circles. Practically a whole day on her own and nothing to show for it. Steven would be back the following morning after a trip south to look over a stud stallion with impeccable blood lines.

The taxi set her down at her hotel and she paid off her fare. Since ten o'clock that morning she had gone everywhere she could think of to locate Liane, making endless prior telephone calls to save the footwork. But all for nothing. The day had gone badly, almost abortive. Her investigations had yielded next to nothing. All she had been able to establish was that Miss Liane Marten had handed in her resignation to the Education Department almost two months previous to the day. She was no longer at her old flat, but she left a forwarding address for her mail which turned out to be no more than a suburban post office box number on the other side of town.

Andrea had taken a bus out and was speaking to the postmaster, a youngish man with keen wrinkles around alert, friendly eyes: Miss Marten had called for the only mail that had been forwarded to that box number and that had been a good five or six weeks before. He had described her perfectly. There could have been no mistake ... tall and very pretty, copper-coloured hair, blue eyes and a nice sprinkling of freckles! ... It was Liane. Only at the last moment had his assistant, a woman, supplied a piece of information, "an idea only" that Miss Marten lived in the old block of flats at the corner of Ashburn Street a few stops back on the bus route. She could have sworn she had seen Miss Marten come out of there one morning on her way to work.

Andrea decided to follow it up. She had gone back to Ashburn Street, only to find no Marten listed on the mail boxes. Going a step further, she had knocked on the door of one of the flats and heard the sound of a television soap opera. A pleasant-faced middle-aged woman had come to the door and listened to her story of looking for a friend with slight interest. It was apparent she wanted to get back to her programme. But for the tiniest moment Andrea fancied she saw a gleam of recognition, a faint darkening flush on the woman's face as she described Liane, but in the next second it was gone and Andrea had turned away with the feeling of failure strong in her.

But for her own personal dilemma she might have given up, but Liane owed her an explanation at least. She had never come forward, rather she had allowed everyone to believe that Andrea had been connected with Carl Godden. She controlled a slight shudder, unwilling to think ill of a dead man, but never in a million years would she have fallen a victim to Carl Godden's unscrupulous

167

brand of charm, the slightly dissolute air that would have hardened and coarsened with age. Liane had – badly, to the point where she had been obsessed with him to the exclusion of everyone else. Yet despite Andrea's private doubts and misgivings, talk of an engagement was in the air. Liane was to accompany Carl on a trip north to his parents' sugar plantation with Andrea a passenger en route for the Barrier Reef for her summer vaction. For some reason neither bothered to explain that Liane had pulled out at the last moment, leaving Andrea in the awkward situation of wanting to cry off with her plans already made.

But she and Liane had shared a friendship that she wished to preserve. Liane thought Carl quite perfect. She would have been bitterly hurt had she known Andrea's true opinion of him, though she could never bring herself to be enthusiastic in any way, hoping the affair would fizzle out given time and a lack of opposition. It was Liane, of course, who had given her the St. Christopher medal the night before Carl Godden's fatal flight into the rain forest inland from the luminous green canefields of his home. Andrea touched a weary hand to her temples. The element of chance that governs one's life! She herself had survived the jungle, survived brain surgery, yet now Liane was missing. But her total disappearance was impossible. It just couldn't be!

Could Liane be living under a false name, and why? It was like knocking one's head against a brick wall. There must be some way of getting around it without starting a full scale inquiry. She could hardly go to the police. Liane never meant her to find her. That was it. But why? What possible defence could she have? Why had she never come forward? Why had she never contacted the Goddens? Why had she allowed everyone to believe Andrea was Carl Godden's fiancée? What purpose did it all serve?

Had she left the country? There were questions without end. None of it seemed to make much sense, yet always Andrea came back to that woman's face at the block of flats, that flick of avidity quickly quenched. Something was wrong there, she felt it in her bones. But was her own vision coloured by her driving need to clear herself of Carl Godden's shadow? Why hadn't she confided in Steven? She knew why. She wanted to tell him herself that there had never been anyone before him and there never would be again.

Steven rang some time after dinner, his voice very crisp and distinct, and pounced immediately on the note of weariness in her voice with a quick: "What's the matter?" She had fended him off, of course, claiming that she had tired herself out walking around the shops. Obviously he disbelieved her, ringing off almost immediately with a very dry: "You might have done better than that, but I'll see you tomorrow!"

She stared down at the phone for some time. What should she have said? Steven, I'm desperately worried. I need you! Must she always run to the man who got things done? Couldn't she handle something on her own? She blinked back tears and prepared for bed, then lay for hours in the dark, trying to fathom a solution before dropping, from sheer tiredness, into a deep, troubled sleep.

In the morning she decided to go back to the flats in Ashburn Street. If she was wrong there was no such thing as a woman's intuition. But for a moment there, that woman's eyes had blazed into life as she described Liane. She would swear to it. Perhaps she had started off on the wrong foot, for the woman had brushed her off like a piece of hot coal. Perhaps Liane was in trouble? Perhaps she had something to hide. Queerly Andrea now began to feel anxiety not for herself, but for the girl she had believed to be her friend.

Her mind flew over the situation and she decided there was no reason why she shouldn't waste an hour or so on a wild goose chase if that was what it was destined to be. If she met with a blank, Steven would be back by midday. By the time she got out of the bus, she was filled with a new sense of drive and direction.

Number 29, Ashburn Street, in the strong morning sunlight, had a ramshackle appearance, an oppressed air. It badly needed painting and the grounds had gone to ruin. She avoided the flat she had tried before, using another entrance. On the ground floor two small children were playing with a kitten and she smiled at them as she felt their wondering eyes as she climbed the stairs to the first floor. No one appeared to be about. The whole place barely looked lived in, musty and nearing its demolition days in a multi-unit zone. No one answered at Flat 3, but she had the impression that someone was watching her. She walked along to Flat 4, a Mrs. Roland. Over and over in her mind she rehearsed what she was going to say, anxious now to have done with it. She pressed the bell. No answer. She waited a few moments, then pressed it again.

Quietly a door opened behind her.

"It's no good ringing the bell *there!*" The voice was ironic, quietly tortured.

Andrea turned with a soft footfall to look across at the young woman framed in the open door, her face deathly white as if she were going to faint. The fine lines of cheek and chin were blurred, the face almost plain with sickness and fatigue.

"Well, well, well!" Andrea said very gently with no thought of effect but a serious, unmelodramatic acceptance.

The girl's face suddenly started to break up, her eyes brimming with tears.

"Andrea, I'm sorry! So sorry!" She came forward haltingly, her hand extended, icy to the touch. "I failed you. I failed myself. I must seem pretty shoddy to you." She searched Andrea's face and found pity, only pity. "Everything was so tragic, so intolerable. How are you, Andrea? I was sick with worry about you. I kept ringing the hospital – you must believe that." She was speaking with anguished difficulty and Andrea slipped an arm about her shoulders with the deepest anxiety, then led her back inside, feeling the chill underlying the warmth of Liane's body.

"I'm all right, now, Liane," she said soothingly. "Don't upset yourself. Is this why you did it?"

"Of course!" Liane tried to smile and her face twisted with pain. "I'm the classic case. You did try to warn me!"

Andrea looked full into the anguished blue yes, the young face out of control, not pretty any more. "Everything's all right now, Lee. You're not alone any more. Now I've found you I'm not likely to lose touch again!" She led the girl into an armchair and lowered her gently into it.

Liane buried her face in her hands. "You don't know what it's been like. Or what it means to me to have a friend again. It's been *hell*! My diagnosis anyway!" She began to laugh and cry all at once, not with hysteria as Andrea knew it but mortal despair.

"Come along now, Liane," Andrea leaned down and patted her hand bracingly. "Don't cry. *Talk*! I'll go and make a cup of tea for you and I'll listen!"

Liane bit on her lip, struggling out of the rip that was sucking her under, and the tears splashed on her hand. Andrea walked through to the tiny kitchen, finding what she wanted quite easily, looking back continuously at Liane. There was nothing of the emotional neurotic about her, enjoying her pain, but age-old suffering womanhood.

Liane began talking, not in highly coloured phrases but clinical detail, talking now as if she could hardly bear a silence, and it came to Andrea she was on the verge of a breakdown. She had battled too long on her own. Her parents were dead. She had no friends – not the real kind anyway. Something had to be done, and soon. She carried the tea back into the living-room and placed a cup in front of Liane, caught up in a sense of pity and sadness.

Liane looked up, half blinded by tears to thank her, and the quality of Andrea's expression suddenly steadied her heart and her hand. She had her old friend back at long last and she never thought the worst of her. She was no longer hopelessly adrift on her own!

When Andrea got back to the hotel, Steven was waiting for her in her sitting-room, his gaze sweeping over her as she walked in, one hand pressed to her head. He stood up tall, and strikingly handsome, weighing her up with a cool, aquamarine gaze. Neither spoke for a moment. Not Andrea first, if a fortune depended on it.

"I've been watching for you!" Steven said at last without expression.

"Oh! I'm late, I know!"

Her delicate face looked paler than usual, her eyes enormous as they always were when she was under any type of stress. For a moment her face was bent forward, her heavy lashes sweeping her cheeks. He made a funny little sound of exasperation, then reached out and tipped

172

up her chin.

"I'm trying very hard to be civilised and reasonable, little one, so please tell me what's been happening to you? It's obvious something's wrong!"

"I found her!" she said, her beautiful eyes quiet and sad on his face.

He hit a hand to his forehead. "I'm good, but I'm not that good! Try again!"

"Liane. Carl Godden's fiancée."

"God!" His eyes suddenly blazed and his hands closed over her shoulders. "Say that again. The quicker the better!"

She repeated it slowly in a strangely different voice, wondering if he knew he was hurting her, but it was an exquisite pain. "We've got to help her, Steven," she said in an intense little voice. "She's sick and she's penniless and she's pregnant!"

His dark face tautened. "Is that so unusual with a type like Godden? He had a callous hand with women, you know."

"Liane had no idea of it," she said sincerely. "She loved him, genuinely loved him. Women in love don't rationalise, Steven. They don't look left and right, they just plunge ahead if their emotions are deeply involved!"

"So what next?" His eyes met hers squarely.

"Instant help! She's dangerously low in spirits and her living conditions are depressing to say the least. There can't be much delay. Pregnancy isn't a premise in the mind and Liane is a physical fact. She's not looking after herself as she should."

He absorbed all this in silence, nodding his dark head. His eyes were vividly intent upon her, but they were strangely masked. "You've remembered everything, haven't you?"

"Yes, I have!"

"Yet you never said anything. I find that curiously hard to accept – almost unforgivable!"

Her eyes swept over his face with a mixture of pleading and challenge. "I thought I was acting for the best, Steven. I wanted to present you with accomplished facts."

His eyes were still veiled, his face enigmatic. "Why not?" he asked with self-mockery. "You're a riddle to me, little one, in lots of ways. As for the other, I'm not really surprised. I never could accept the idea of you and Godden. In fact, I couldn't bear to give it any credence at all. You've got an inherent fastidiousness that would protect you from his type."

"He's dead, Steven!" she said quietly.

His eyes went over her head, then he dropped his hands and walked over to look out the window, lighting a cigarette.

"The Goddens mightn't be the perfect solution for your friend, but at least they have a right to know about their coming grandchild, and the girl has the right to financial assistance if nothing else. The future for an unmarried woman with a child isn't quite as grim as it used to be. Does she intend to keep the child when it comes?"

"I hadn't the heart to ask her – one thing at a time. But she loved Carl desperately. I can't imagine her wanting to give up her own flesh and blood. All she wants to do now is escape the scene of failure and disgrace, for that's how she's seeing things at the moment!"

Their eyes locked for a moment and a curious glint came into his blue-green eyes, lighting his dark, forceful face. "It's easy enough to help her in that way, tide her over her time and a good while after. But I can't help thinking the Goddens have a responsibility in this matter, neither do I think them callous enough to evade it. One more thing, and an important one – I want you cleared of Carl Godden's image!"

Andrea stood transfixed, pinned by some quality in his expression. Then he smiled, his white teeth very attractive in his dark face. "Don't panic, honey!"

"You've never called me that before!" she said a little breathlessly.

"And it's not like me either!" he said with a flicker of sardonic humour.

She stood there staring at him, her eyes clinging to him instinctively as if for support. He looked across at her face and gave a brief laugh.

"This isn't helping Liane any! Now why don't you let me sort out the final details in my mind while you have a rest? I haven't got you on your feet to see you played out again with someone else's problems. We'll lunch about two, then you can take me back to meet your friend!"

She seemed to be looking at him in an unbreathing stillness as if he were the ageless source of energy and dynamism. "Will *you* contact Irina Godden?" she asked huskily, the colour of her eyes deepening into an intense grey. "She ruined her son, you know!"

"I think it unlikely she would attempt the same thing with a grandson. Life teaches us some things, even if it is in the hardest way possible. Anyway, I could let them know the position and take it from there. The girl could always assume another name, make a life for herself with adequate financial support. But leave it to me. You're all eyes!" He shot back his cuff and looked at his watch. "You have an hour before I take you to lunch. Make the most of it!" He moved so suddenly that it gave her a queer sense of vertigo. She swayed a little and to regain her balance clutched out at his arm instinctively.

175

"Steven!"

She sounded like a wounded bird. His arm shot around her and Andrea looked up at him quickly, catching her breath. His eyes were narrow, glittering with laughter.

"So simple! So natural! Too simple by half!" He bent his head, his lips brushing her cheek, then with sudden decision closing on her mouth quick and hard. Before her mind had dealt with the situation he was at the door, moving with long soundless paces. "A sorceress innocent of her own devices!" he said dryly. "Now get up on the bed and have a rest!" The irony in his voice was so gentle it was a subtle caress. She made a curious little sound and he smiled and shut the door, leaving her to slip off her dress and tuck a pillow under her head.

It took Irina Godden the space of a thousand-mile jet flight from North Queensland to arrive in the State capital. Andrea, when she saw her again, was appalled. The woman had undergone a drastic alteration in appearance. Immaculately groomed as ever, age had fallen on her almost overnight. It was then that Andrea truly realised the extent of the unhappiness Irina Godden had borne.

The afternoon had been hectic. Liane's hair had to be washed and set and Andrea had torn out in a frantic rush to buy something pretty and becoming for Liane to wear, depressed beyond words with what she had been making do with, saving what little money she had. Now Steven had gone out to the airport to meet Irina and the two girls sat in a tense, waiting silence, Andrea at a loss for more than desultory conversation, Liane feeling too sick to focus her mind. Already she had been ill twice, with nervous tension, and she gave another gasp and turned her white face to Andrea.

"I'm going to be sick again!"

"You're damn well *not*!" Andrea spoke so emphatically the other girl sat down again. "Try and get a grip of yourself, Lee. Irina's made a commendable response to the situation, you must realise that. She'll be here on the first possible flight. I pray it's every bit as good as it appears to be on the face of it!"

"I'm so bitterly ashamed for her to see me like this!" Liane muttered.

"Now, Lee, you look very nice – and don't tell me you don't or I'll be offended. It won't help all these recriminations. You'll only make yourself ill and you can't change anything. And don't think I don't know it's easy to talk! When the baby arrives all this unhappiness will be over. It's going to be the most wonderful baby in the whole wide world and you're going to lavish your love on it and wonder how you ever lived without your little son or your little daughter."

Liane was looking down at her locked hands. "She mightn't be like you, Andrea. You're my friend and you've known me a long time. You know what sort of person I really am!"

"Oh, Lee, don't talk like that, Irina Godden is a mature woman and she's seen a great deal of life – and life in the torrid zone at that. She won't go around moralising, I'm sure. Your welfare will be her first priority and that of her coming grandchild. It's exactly the same procedure for all of us from start to finish. The only variant is you lack the privileges and security only marriage can give!"

"We *would* have been married, Andy!" The blue eyes began to brim again with a measure of quiet desperation.

"Yes, of course, dear!" Not for the life of her would Andrea have said anything else. "Don't cry again. You'll only redden your eyes and you want to look your best!"

Both girls gave a wry grimace at that and Liane sat

back, trying to make a little conversation. They didn't have to wait long after that. There was the sound of footsteps outside the door, then Steven opened it out, the general tension not lost on him as he allowed Irina Godden to precede him into the room. She walked in slowly but without hesitation, greeted Andrea with a certain warmth and dignity, but her eyes were for the copper-haired Liane, who sat, chin up, blushing painfully.

"My dear!" the older woman went forward on a note of swift impulsiveness with no trace of bitterness or embarrassment in her voice. The feeling of relief and well-being that swept through Andrea quite startled her with its force. Liane too betrayed her natural reaction, her warm, generous mouth trembled.

Irina turned to Steven and Andrea with a face that had grown anxious and eager. "Would you mind if I spoke to Liane alone? I know I have a great deal to thank you both for. As I told Steven on my way here, I would never have forgiven myself if I turned my back on my grandchild or its mother, and Nick feels the same way. I suppose it's because a child stakes out its own claim, wanted or not. The longed-for first-born, the ... unexpected. They're all entitled to our love and protection. Liane and I will work something out. I must confess it's not what I wanted or hoped for, but at this stage of my life I've come to terms with human nature. That Carl and Liane didn't have the opportunity to marry ... well!" she stumbled and broke down, then recovered herself with a toss of her head. "People will talk, but there's always something new to occupy their interest and one can't allow one's life to be governed by what people think. For all my faults I've never done *that*! To feel is the thing. I'd like to take Liane back with me. In some ways the plantation is the end of the world, and she would suffer
178

very few embarrassments. Or I'll see to it that she's adequately looked after here. It's for Liane to decide!"

"Well then," Steven said briskly, "we'll leave you to it. May I say, Mrs. Godden, I hope you find in your grandchild a compensating balance for your loss. Your attitude does you great credit."

She looked at him and smiled with a humility she had rarely shown in her whole life. "I do hope you're right, Steven. And now, my dear ...!" She glanced down at Liane's bent head and Steven quietly took Andrea's arm and drew her out of the room, shutting the door on them.

"Everything's going to be all right!" Andrea leaned against the wall with a sigh of relief.

He suddenly swept his hand over her pale, shining head. "It would seem so! At any rate the situation has vastly improved. Now do you think we could have a little time to ourselves? Irina has the suite, so she'll make out all right and I would say, at a guess, that Liane has fallen on her feet at long last. How long do you think it would take you to dress for dinner? I thought we might take a run down the Coast. It'll only take an hour and I know all the best places to eat. Quite frankly, with all these good works, I'm starving!"

She smiled and her eyes showed a hundred pinpoints of light. "Fifteen minutes?"

He looked at her reprovingly – tall, faintly teasing, diabolically self-assured. "I suppose ten would be making things too easy for me?"

"I'll see!"

At the time they were talking, Andrea was being paged in the foyer and when she reached her room the phone was beginning to ring again. She went to it quickly with the horrible sinking sensation that it might be Helena trying to locate Steven. No one else she could think of would

179

be likely to ring her unless it was Room Service.

"Andrea Swanson here!" she said clearly into the mouthpiece with the gallant performance of a young woman with not a care in the world.

"Switchboard, Miss Swanson–" a pert young voice said, equally carefree. "We're holding a trunk call for you now. I'll connect you with your party. Tempe Downs calling."

Andrea relaxed with an audible sigh and sank down on the bed as she heard Luke Freedman's pleasant drawl.

"Hello, Andrea, how are you? The third time today I've tried to contact you!"

"I've been out a lot, Luke!" The smile sounded in her voice. "How lovely to hear your voice again. You got my letter?"

"I did, my dear, and very charming and welcome it was too. A little bit of gossip before business," he drawled confidentially. "Allowing for professional discretion, 'you know who' has resigned from the hospital committee!"

He smiled at the faint gasp that came over the wire. "Would you believe it?"

It took a moment for Andrea to regain herself. "Good grief! Did she give a reason?"

"A slight one. She's joining her dear mamma on the Continent!"

"How jolly!" Andrea's voice turned very dry. "Do you need a replacement?"

"I'll come to that," he said comfortably, "but first I have a job lined up for you a little sooner than I thought. It seems the ideal situation to me, but naturally I wanted to hear what you think. A little patient of mine is being discharged next week after a bout of rheumatic fever. Her people have quite a big property on the Western

180

Downs. At any rate she won't be going back to boarding school this year. She's nearly ten, in the fifth grade – a very nice child. Much too delicate of course, but very bright. No trouble at all to teach, I should think. You know what's coming, of course – a spot of governessing. I know her parents would be delighted to get anyone with your qualifications. I've skirted around the preliminaries, but I wanted to discuss it with you first. What do you say?"

His voice was friendly and eager and enthusiastic all at once. It was very difficult indeed to keep the sudden desolation out of her voice. "It sounds very suitable, Luke," she said, swallowing hard. "When would I have to start?" What did it matter when she started? she thought desolately. She could never go back to Mokhana. Like Vivienne before her Helena might, in the end, prove too much for her. Luke had already said a dozen words before she heard him clearly "... discuss that with the child's mother. I know she'd be more than ready to meet you half way. She has a genuine simplicity and warmheartedness I know you'll find attractive!"

He must have been finding her reaction disappointing, for there was a hesitation, then his voice, quietly interrogative.

"Andrea?"

"Still here, Luke!" She tried to inject enthusiasm into her voice. "I'm just thinking things over. It's very kind of you to think of me. There's so much really I could tell you. I mentioned in my letter about the medal, but a great deal has happened since then. Every last little piece of my memory has fallen into place!"

A new excitement tingled through him, but he held himself against it. "That's wonderful, Andrea!" he said with deep sincerity. "I was hoping for something like that.

181

Selective amnesias usually respond to stimulus, and you had quite a few things working against you at the beginning. You must tell me all about it when I see you. You're coming to Bynyara, of course?"

Andrea was suddenly staring into a future without Steven. She hadn't properly faced it before. "About that, Luke," she said carefully, "I don't know!"

"But you *will*, my dear!" Luke's voice sounded gay and confident, "if I have to partner you myself!"

Her eyes circled restlessly about the room. "You sound very determined, Luke. But a complication has arisen not altogether unforeseen!"

"Oh!" The single syllable was loaded with comprehension.

"I wonder if you do, Luke," she said quietly.

"I think so, my dear. I know the old stories."

She looked down at her wrist watch, the minutes ticking away. "May I ring you back about this, Luke? Steven is waiting for me and he's not a man to keep waiting. I'd like to discuss the job with him if I may. He's been so very good to me I must consult him on it."

"By all means, my dear!" He made a not very successful attempt to keep the wry resentment out of his voice. "And Andrea?"

"Yes, Luke!"

"I'm looking forward to at least three dances at Bynyara!"

Her eyes were very gentle, softly contemplative. "If I'm there, you shall have them — that's a promise. Until tomorrow, Luke!"

"Good night, my dear!"

The phone clicked with finality and Andrea put the receiver down. She felt a little dazed, utterly resigned. Events were moving quickly now. By tomorrow she would have to make her decision, though in reality the decision had been made for her long ago. She could never go back to Mokhana, Helena's stronghold. Somehow people never got treated the way they deserved. Helena was Steven's aunt. She loved him in her fashion. In a sense, she had shown him a lifetime's devotion. More crushing, Helena had made the certain claim that he would never betray her. It was true, another harsh fact she would have to face. But she had tonight!

She pulled her dress over her head and reached into the wardrobe for white brocade evening culottes patterned in silver and gold thread. They made the most of her pale gold tan and were suitable for dining out on the Gold Coast. She zipped the low back and kicked off her shoes, stepped into strappy gold sandals, then hurried over to the dressing-table and slipped a gold bracelet on her arm and matching ear-rings. Fortunately her make-up was still impeccable, for she had little time to attend to that. She picked up her hair brush and swirled her silver-gilt hair into a shining aureole. It was growing out quickly now. She pulled a few tendrils on to her cheek-bones, her ear-rings making little golden triangles in the hollows.

She hovered a moment more uncertainly, then she fetched out her evening bag and walked to the door, flicking off the lights as she went. The room was plunged into instant purple gloom. She threw open the door and her heart quivered with shock. Steven caught her upraised arm just above the elbow, his voice threaded with lazy vitality.

"There's no need to spring away like a startled faun. You *did* say fifteen minutes. Even if twenty was worth it!"

His dark head was clearly defined against the glimmering lights of the corridor. He looked disturbingly handsome strange yet familiar in a beautiful suit she had never seen. His brilliant gaze was slipping over her face and shoulders, the slight, singing line of her body.

"Well?" He could feel the warmth and the scent of her, his eyes twin points of light.

"I had an unexpected phone call. It held me up a bit!" she explained rather helplessly, in some odd way feeling closer to him than she had ever been before.

"Oh!" The non-committal exclamation still demanded a quick answer.

"Luke Freedman," she supplied apologetically, wondering why she should answer that way.

He drew her right out into the light, his eyes downright hostile, a dangerous winged slant to his brows.

"Now why in the world would Freedman be ringing you?"

She experienced a powerful compulsion to hurt him as much as he was hurting her. "Do I really have to go in to that? I like him and he likes *me*!"

His voice was very dry, clinical and detached, yet he was holding her to the point of pain. "But he doesn't *like* you, Andrea. You're all he thinks about in between appendicectomies and snakebite and difficult confinements!"

She gave a choked little indrawn breath. "There's absolutely no need to be unkind!"

"Let's say Freedman brings out the worst in me!"

"And I thought that was my prerogative?"

She heard his terse, arrogant tones:

"So it *is*, most of the time!"

She felt utterly forlorn, yet his fascination survived in some strange way. "If you're going to be like this, Steven, I'm not going at all!"

"Aren't you?"

He turned on her then, the expression on his handsome face, the exact tone of his voice a masterpiece of ironic disbelief. Panic was the swiftest stimulant of all. He looked a hard, dangerous man, yet he couldn't drive out her desire to oppose him.

"All right, then!" she said recklessly. "But don't say I didn't warn you!"

His eyes flickered over her in the most baffling way. He gave a brief sardonic laugh. "It's getting that way I fear to turn my back on you. You seem to attract trouble as a matter of course. But to resurrect an old question ... what *did* Freedman ring you for?"

She gave a small bewildered exclamation. "I can see you're going to worry this to death. I'll tell you in the car if you can wait that long. Patience doesn't seem to be your number one asset!"

"And you're so right!" He gave her a long considering look but didn't say anything further, moving back to the lift to jab a finger to the button. They descended, in silence, to the basement, then walked to the bay where Steven had parked a late model hire car. Five minutes later they were out under the stars. It was a soft, balmy night with a breeze, still warm enough in early May to go without a wrap.

Steven drove swiftly out of the city, into the suburbs, seemingly preoccupied with finding the shortest possible route to the Highway. They were well on to it before he flickered a glance over her slightly averted profile, very chaste, very remote.

"You might start at the beginning, Andrea, if you don't mind!" His tone was soft but uncompromising. "I've all the time in the world and I find the subject quite fascinating!"

She flattened her back against the plush upholstery.

"Luke has a job lined up for me!" She allowed herself one brief glance at his profile.

"There now!" His voice was heavily spiced with sarcasm. "She produces it almost like a ventriloquist's dummy. And what in sweet hell are you discussing jobs with Luke Freedman for?"

She could feel his anger pressing in on her like a physical weight. "You can't mean that, Steven. My convalescence is over. I can't rely on your resources for ever! Every damn thing I've got, you bought. I had every intention of discussing it with you. You must know how grateful . . ."

"Stop it!" he bit out between clenched teeth. "Don't ever, now or never, mention the word *gratitude* to me. You owe me nothing. If you weren't so damned odd, you'd be interesting. Why precisely do you need a job at this point? And *why* from Freedman?"

"I've got to eat!" she said a little wildly. She didn't seem to know what to do with her hands, so she clenched them tightly in her lap.

His face was set in lines of dark anger. "I haven't noticed you starving these past few months!"

Her eyes deepened and darkened, the pupils encroaching on the ring of grey. "You're impossible, aren't you, Steven!"

She sounded so melodramatic that his mouth relaxed, very near smiling. "It happens to be my second baptismal name and I won't change!"

Her expression was now openly mutinous, her voice brittle and challenging. "You're telling me! Pull over, I'm getting out!"

"A not unworthy suggestion, but you're definitely not getting *out*!"

His dry voice quenched her rising agitation. She sub-

186

sided at once. He pulled the car off the road and slid it into the tree-lined shadows with the sombre monotones of a charcoal drawing. Andrea felt a little shiver pass through her body. In the confined space of the car she felt a stifling sense of imprisonment and a dark rush of excitement. Steven in this mood posed an element of danger. He switched off the engine and slid his arm along the back of the seat, almost but not quite touching her.

"You're not going to bolt like a scared little rabbit. I want to hear all about this job of yours. It seems to me Freedman is giving a whole lot of advice."

She lifted her face, willing herself out of the tremors that gripped her. "I'm not private property, am I? Trespassing not allowed!"

His eyes slid over her softly, gleaming with speculation.

"It looks rather like it though, doesn't it?"

Her hands formed themselves into small fists yet she felt shaken and weak. She loved him so much, she *hated* him! His arrogance and his strength, the soft irony of his voice, the glance that slid over her as if he had a perfect right to look at her however he pleased. To stay within range of that unwavering scrutiny was becoming intolerable. She turned her head quickly with a blinding sense of injustice.

"You're looking at this the wrong way, Steven," she said, trying to hold her voice down to calm reasonableness. "Luke is only trying to help me. I can't stay on Mokhana for ever. I have to make my own way!"

His mouth hardened and he said with a cool passion that utterly shook her:

"You move me to tears! All right, little one, if we're to understand each other. I've always intended you to stay on Mokhana right from the start. Swear if you can you

187

didn't know it. And if you *can't*, don't let me have any missish manoeuvres now!" He flung up an imperious hand. "I'm *still* waiting to hear about this job of yours!"

"For God's sake, why the interest? It's governessing, if you must know. A small patient of Luke's is going home next week – a nine-year-old girl. I should be able to manage *that*, seeing that Luke doesn't think I should go back to full-time teaching yet!"

A flash of quick anger crossed his face, but his voice was cool: "So he's reached that conclusion, has he? I always forget he's the doctor! Can you *really* see yourself as the little governess at the back of beyond with Luke Freedman dancing attendance every other free week-end off?"

"Yes, damn it, I *can*!" His insolence was unforgivable, sparking her own anger.

"Well, think again!" His voice dropped dangerously low. She arched away from him with a convulsive little movement. "Don't you touch me, Steven!"

His continuing silence was matched by the still severity of his dark face. It seemed to punish her for her temerity. How dared she talk back to the great Steven Daintree! Her mouth started to tremble. "Everything you do. What you say. Everything about you ... you're *swamping* me, Steven. You're ..."

Her voice strange and haunted was brutally cut off. He jerked her into his arms and brought down his mouth, kissing her in a way she was never likely to forget. Her body, unprompted, made a frantic move to elude him, but he held her implacably, his hands travelling over her with great sureness, an authority in his touch that gradually transmuted resistance to a boneless quiescence. A lightning transition from unhappiness to a miraculous submission. She closed her eyes and turned up her mouth,

188

feeling her doubts and her fears and her resentments buried deep beneath a trancelike enchantment. She had no aim, no desire, no will to do anything but go on feeling this dazzling, white-hot excitement like a thousand-volt shock through every nerve in her body. She abandoned all pretence and moved against him.

He jerked up his head, a brittle little smile on his mouth.

"I can't stand much more of this, nor can you. It's about time you had someone to sleep with you!"

Her free hand touched the smooth nape of his neck. "You don't *have* to say that, Steven. You've proved it all. I'm no thinking person in your arms, I know that. I want you as much as you say you want me, but there's a difference – the all-important distinction. I *love* you too!"

His dark-timbred voice seemed to hold a faint taunt: "And you think I don't know that?"

"Why should you not? I'm not sophisticated enough to hide my needs. And my need for you is basic. Critical, I suppose, almost necessary for my survival. To be without you would be like getting lost in the jungle again – worse maybe. You have to *be* lost to know what it's like." She suddenly put her hands over her eyes like a pathetic child. "Loving is not just this tide of passion, it's tenderness and caring and wanting to share things. *Everything*. Pitiful, aren't I? I can't go on!"

He pulled her hands away from her face and locked them in one of his own. "Andrea, I could beat you!"

"Could you? How odd!"

It was impossible to read his expression. He lifted his head and looked out over the night. "And you don't think I feel that way about you?"

Andrea traced a finger over the curve of his mouth. "*Tell* me, Steven. But you won't. The price for loving

189

comes too high. You won't talk."

"And you talk too much!" He bent his head and kissed her mouth hard. "I love you, you little fool. I want you in every way a man can – to make love to, I can't deny *that*. But you happen to possess a very special grace for me. I want you beside me day in and day out, not just all the nights of my life. I want to know that you're there wherever I turn, to hear your soft voice, know your charm and your humour, that deep vein of compassion, even those odd little bursts of temper!"

She had her head tilted back, listening to his beautifully inflected voice, her eyes a silvery dazzle in the half light. Though she shied away from it passionately she had to come out with the name that cut close to the centre of her thoughts.

"And Helena?"

He ran his hand through her silky hair and tugged her head gently from side to side. "Do you think I'm fool enough to let history repeat itself? I would never ask my wife to share her home with a woman who was actively hostile to her. Helena is leaving Mokhana. She'll take no more than a few days to find something she considers suitable. Naturally I'll continue to support her in exactly the same way. It's very difficult for me to be harsh to a woman who has always shown me loyalty and love – of a kind. But Helena came to me about you the night before we left. It was all rather cruel and unpleasant but necessary. She has her own pride. She'll make her way."

He touched her throat with a softly tender gesture. "It might be difficult for you to understand, little one, but Helena and my father shared a rather harsh upbringing, in a sense. My grandfather was a wealthy man, but he had a few notable eccentricities. One of them was to bring up his children in the military fashion – lots of rules and regulations, skills to be acquired, duty first and demonstrations of love not at all. It affected them both in later life. I loved my own father and admired him, but he was a hard man, I remember that – as hard in his fashion as my mother was sensitive. It's very difficult for a child to judge an adult situation. I was at boarding school most of the time and when I came home my father always had some kind of safari arranged for us both. Then too, I had the heritage of Mokhana. There was always so much to learn. I never had much time with my mother, but it was enough for me to know she was there. I'll never let you run away from me, little one. Not *ever*. Remember that!"

"And your mother?" Andrea asked softly.

"Leave it!" he said gently. She could see from the expression on his face that his memories were bitter ones. He was not ready to cope with it yet. He looked down at her suddenly as if he caught the very drift of her thoughts. "You seem to be changing the very pattern of my life. It was never intended that you should leave me – a silver-haired, silver-eyed slip of a girl who's entered into my bloodstream." He traced a finger over her delicate profile and she shivered like a cool stream of air playing over her face and throat. It was very quiet about them as if a blanket had come down on all sound.

His voice was very low and caressing, turning her heart over. "I've no intention of wasting a great deal of time before I do something about it. There is such a thing as a special licence." He curved his hand under her chin and turned her face up. "Tell me right now before I go another mile. How long do I have to wait?"

She stretched up her hand and turned her palm against his mouth, feeling a torrent of love close over her head. "A few days. A week. I don't know about these things.

Whenever you like, Steven!"

For a half a minute he continued to look down at her face, then he lowered his head ...

When finally Andrea leaned away from him she asked breathlessly, staring into his eyes brushed with moonlight and her own heady exultation, "What shall I do about Luke?"

He threw back his head in the old arrogant fashion, shifting his arm that lay behind her head, leaning forward to turn on the ignition.

"Why, nothing, my love. I'll ring him in the morning. But don't worry, I'll let him down very gently, as painlessly as possible. But I really see no necessity to have a working wife!"

She didn't move, didn't say anything. She just turned her head along the seat, letting her eyes play over his imperious dark head, the purely cut profile, the line of his mouth indescribably softened to tenderness. It was a picture burned for ever into her mind's eye, intruding into the thought and shape of her dreams.

The car pulled back on to the road and the wind whispered enticingly. They were speeding through the night of windy stars and a curved sickle moon. She moved closer to him, feeling his dark strength and vitality. She was moving into a future she had counted for ever lost.